Basic Living

G.M. Whitley

Copyright © 2013 G.M. Whitley

All rights reserved.

This is a work of fiction
and any resemblance between the characters and persons
living or dead is purely coincidental.

ISBN-10: 149220627X
ISBN-13: 978-1492206279

For my wonderful family. Thank you for supporting my writing habit.

HENRY

These people write a check so they can feel good about themselves, that they've done something to help the poor. They don't actually care about us except in the abstract. They don't want to know us or interact with us. Maybe on Thanksgiving they will go into a Basic Living ward to serve a meal. Around Christmas they will adopt a BL family and teach their children the importance of helping the needy by buying a cart full of plastic toys and adorable clothes. Then they return to their comfortable lives without having to think about us for a good long while.

Of course, I am fully aware that I have become Them. Did I buy a home anywhere near the BL ward? Of course not. Do I want my kids playing with BL kids? No way. Do I send a check to the Keller Schools every year? I do. We even adopt five f—king BL families at Christmas.

Excerpt from My Life after Basic Living, by essayist Felicia Webb, The New Yorker, 5/18/2043.

Henry wasn't allowed to come home until the street lights turned on. This wouldn't have been a problem if he had friends, but Henry much preferred solitude. If he stayed in the school playground much past four o'clock, the guards would make him leave. Loitering wasn't allowed in the BL ward. If the cops found him hanging out in an alley, he would be taken to the Boys & Girls Club. Henry did go there for a while, but the workers wouldn't let him be. They wanted him to talk to them, to interact with the other kids. To play air hockey or basketball or board games. Henry didn't want any of that. He just wanted to watch.

He saw things other people didn't see. Like the way his history teacher's hair part was a little crooked, just like her front teeth. Or the pattern of cracks in the concrete under the jungle gym, the little weeds forcing their way upward. The tiny flecks of green embedded under his mother's fingernails after a day at the algae processing plant, no matter how much she scrubbed them. How the sadness never left her face, even when she was blissed out.

At first he tried sitting at the end of the hall, but he couldn't bear to watch the men come and go from their apartment. He had learned his lesson about trying to stop it years ago. The social worker couldn't do anything but send his mom to rehab. It didn't work. The next step was jail or Sanctuary, but if she went he would end up in a BL group home. It would be as bad as the Boys & Girls Club. Maybe worse. So they just pretended that everything was OK, and as long as his mom was able to meet her work requirements, they would be fine. But he still wasn't allowed to come home until the street lights turned on.

Fortunately, Henry had finally found the perfect spot. He made a deal with the maintenance guy of his building. In exchange for the code to get through the door to the roof, Henry used his points to buy chocolate bars for the guy. His wife made him use all his points on canned fruit and vegetables. Henry wasn't good in school, but he was always on time and never a discipline problem, so he got his points regularly. The roof even had a little utility shed he could hole up in when it was rainy.

He still stayed after school on Tuesdays. There was a twenty-minute window when the students were all gone and the teachers were in meetings. Henry went from room to room to scrounge materials from the trash. He always started with the kindergarten class since they were the only ones who did arts and crafts. He stacked discarded papers and carefully stashed them in his backpack. He took all the broken pencils. He had bottles and bottles of paints with only a dab left in the bottom. He had a box filled to the brim with tiny bits of broken crayon and dried out markers that he soaked in water to coax back to life. He never took anything from the cupboards. He knew better.

Henry stored his supplies under the bed with his most treasured possession of all, an art history textbook he found at the Don. Somebody must have cleared out an attic and donated everything because there was a whole shelf of outdated textbooks. It had taken him four months to save the points. He visited the Don every day, in agony until he confirmed that the book was still there. When it was finally his, Henry had taken it home and cried. He hadn't cried since he was six.

Henry read the book every night. The artist's names were like magic to him. He drew every painting over and over, until his work was as close as he could get using his materials. He went back to his old drawings after that, embarrassed at how childish they were. He threw them all away and started again. He worked from his memory. His classmates at a table at lunch. The field trip to the AlgiPro processing plant in eighth grade. He drew the inside of the utility shed. The hanging tools. The work bench. He drew the view from the rooftop. He drew abstract images, pouring his emotions onto the backs of old homework assignments.

Henry was sitting against the utility shed, his supplies neatly arranged on the gravel-coated asphalt, when he heard the maintenance man walk up.

"Hey, Mr. Bautista," Henry said. He reached into his backpack and pulled out a Snickers bar. "Here you go."

"Thanks." Mr. Bautista peeled back the wrapper and took a single bite. He slowly chewed and swallowed, then put the rest in his jumpsuit pocket. "See you next week."

"Um," Henry said. "Uh."

"Yeah? Spit it out, kid."

"I was wondering if I could paint the shed. On the inside, so nobody would see it."

"It doesn't need to be painted."

"Not like that. Like this." Henry held out the drawing he had been working on, his hand trembling a little.

"You drew this?" Mr. Bautista looked skeptical.

"Yeah," Henry said. "I draw lots of stuff."

"I don't have any paint you can use."

"I got my own."

"You steal it?"

"No. From the trash at school. I been saving it up for a while now. I have enough to do this."

"Show me where you want to paint."

They went into the utility shed.

"That wall there," Henry said. It was the back wall. Plain plywood.

"That paint going to show up right on the wood?"

"I don't know," Henry said.

"What if you do it at my place?"

"What?" Henry asked.

"You do it at my place. The wall in our bedroom is white. Yeah. Mrs. Bautista would like that."

"Really?"

"You do it like this?" Mr. Bautista held up the paper.

"Yeah, but bigger."

"How long it gonna take you?"

"I don't know. Never done anything that big before. Maybe a week. Maybe less. If I do after school and all day Saturday and Sunday."

"OK."

"OK?"

"You start tomorrow? I keep this to show her? Make sure it's what she wants."

Henry hesitated. "I never let nobody keep my stuff."

"You need it to do your big painting, right? We keep it safe."

"I could bring it back tomorrow after school."

"Mrs. Bautista will be at work then."

"I could come now."

"She at work now."

"I'll bring it when she gets home. My mom will let me go anytime." Henry reached out for the paper. Mr. Bautista reluctantly gave it back.

"She get home at ten. Apartment 224."

"OK."

Mr. Bautista left. It was almost dark so Henry packed up all his things and took the stairs down to their apartment. It was a studio. Deemed large enough for a single mother with kid. They had a microwave for the BL packs and a mini-fridge for his milk. Henry stopped at the door and listened. He heard low talking, like the TV built into the wall was on.

"Hey Mom," Henry said, opening the door.

"Hey Henry," she said. "Mike's here! He's staying for dinner."

Henry sighed. This meant Mom would skip dinner tomorrow night. She never would let Henry share his. Mike was the closest thing she had to a boyfriend, but he never brought anything to them. He was a big guy who worked the BL construction crew by day and was an amateur fighter by night. Mike was pretty good at the fighting, so it wasn't like he lacked points to get extra food. He didn't need to take theirs.

Henry's eyes adjusted to the dim lighting panels in the ceiling. Mom and Mike were cuddled up on her bed. Mike was leafing through Henry's book. His book. Henry froze. Had he left it out? He couldn't remember. Had Mike gone through his stuff?

"This is pretty cool," Mike said.

"Yeah," Henry replied. He tried to sound nonchalant.

"I like this one a lot," Mike said, tapping a page thoughtfully. "Can I have it, Henry?"

"No."

"Henry, that's rude," his mom said. "It's just one page out of like five hundred. Mike, you can have it."

"It's mine." Henry said. He wondered what would happen if he just grabbed the book and ran.

"You are upsetting me, Henry," Mike said softly. "Do you want to upset me?"

"Henry," his mother cautioned. "Just let him have it."

Mike lifted the page, about to tear it.

"Wait, just wait!" Henry said, holding up both hands, palms outward. "Please. Let me see which one it is first."

Mike held up the book.

"OK." Henry dropped to his knees and rummaged under his bed. He pulled out a sheet of paper. "Here. Here you go. This is it. Take this."

Mike looked back and forth from the book to the paper. He held the book out to Henry with one hand and reached for the paper with the other. "Did you draw this?" Mike asked.

"Yeah," Henry said.

"You know he did this?" Mike asked his mom.

"Henry don't tell me much," his mom said.

"You do more of these?"

Could he get away with a lie?

"Boy, I am asking you a question. You got more of these under that bed? You gonna make me get up?"

"Yes. There's more."

"Let me see."

Henry hesitated.

"I ain't gonna take any more of them, alright? Just this one you gave me. OK?"

"OK." Henry reached under the bed and pulled out the stack. Mike took his time going through them. He asked Henry to show him where the paintings were in the book.

"Now this one ain't in the book," he said, holding up a portrait of Henry's mother, asleep on her bed.

"You drew me, Henry?" she asked.

"You was sleeping. I'm sorry."

"No, it's just... I ain't that pretty."

"You are," Mike said. "You're lovely. These are real good, Henry. Real good. You got some talent there." Mike stood up. He left the drawings on the bed, keeping only the one Henry gave him. "I gotta go."

"I thought you were staying for dinner!" Henry's mom protested.

"I got some stuff to do. Just remembered." Mike kissed her forehead. "I'll be by soon."

VERA AND BOB

Do you view the poor as people born into unfortunate circumstances who have been given little opportunity to overcome their background? Or do you view them as a sub-species of lazy opportunistic parasites who suck money and resources from the hardworking? While the answer for most is nuanced, our political parties have always legislated in black and white. Once you understand that, you will understand why Senator Baxter's Basic Living proposal is the solution.

Jack McCormick, opinion piece for The Atlantic, 2/16/29.

Vera scanned a stack of BL packs, a roll of paper towels, and a bar of soap. She tapped a button. "Print please," she said.

Roxanne pressed her thumb against the scanner. "Late shift tonight?" she asked, putting her rations into a cloth bag.

"Yeah," Vera said. "I'm on till midnight."

"I'm thinking of putting in for a transfer over here," Roxanne said. "KidCare is driving me crazy. One of the little bastards bit me today." Roxanne tugged her sleeve up, revealing a bright red imprint on her upper arm.

"At least you only have to do it three days a week," Vera said. "Aren't you retraining?"

"I quit that. This time they pegged me for domestic help. Like I want to spend the rest of my life cleaning up rich people's shit while they treat me like shit."

"Yeah," Vera said.

"How many points I got?" Roxanne asked.

"Twelve," Vera said, checking Roxanne's Index.

"One cigarette. One lotto ticket," she said.

Vera put in the request. Her manager came over, double-checked Roxanne's Index and completed the transaction. Roxanne's point balance dropped to zero.

"Thanks, Vera. I'll see you next week," Roxanne said. She picked up her bag of rations and headed out of the store. Vera was always surprised at the way people used their points. Booze. Cigarettes. The lotto. She and Bob saved theirs. They usually had enough to get vouchers for McDonald's on their birthdays and anniversary. Their daughter, Jolene, gave them the bus passes to get there and added vouchers for ice cream cones to their Indexes. It was all her husband would let her do. They were scraping by on his salary and the daycare Jolene ran at their rental house.

Their son, Bob Jr., was in prison for armed robbery. Idiot boy didn't understand that pretty much everything was recorded on crystal these days. He took out the cameras at the jewelry store, but was caught by a host of others at neighboring stores and streetlights. Jolene sent bus passes for a yearly visit to him too.

And Charlie. Their youngest. Poor Charlie Peaced Out when he was twenty-five. He started hearing voices when he was sixteen. After finishing high school, he went on BL and worked the algae pools. He saw the BL psychiatrist and got some prescriptions, but nothing helped. When he was twenty-two, Charlie flipped out and nearly drowned the guy working next to him, convinced there was a monster in the pools. His manager sent him to Sanctuary. Drugged to the gills, Charlie waited three years for a spot to open up at a charitable Enclave. Finally, he decided enough was enough.

Vera had gone with him to the Peace Out Center in Nashville. It was on a sprawling horse farm and the mares had just foaled. It was the nicest place either of them had ever stayed. Vera still had dreams about the lavish bedrooms and meals. As for Charlie, she was just glad she didn't have to worry about him anymore. They kept his ashes in an urn under the bed.

Vera and Bob ended up on BL after the factory closed. They drained their savings during the year Bob spent looking for work. Nobody wanted or needed a sixty-year-old blue collar guy with his best days behind him. He got a job stocking groceries part-time at the Kroger where Vera worked as a checker, but even their combined income wasn't enough to keep them off BL, not with their health issues.

Vera scanned the next customer's BL packs, a gallon of milk, and a box of diapers. Only the ones with kids got real milk. The mom had a boy in tow and he was screaming his head off. She dully apologized. Vera gave her the understanding mother nod. Even though the kid had to be two, the mom kept trying to stick a pacifier in his mouth. He bit her hand and she gave up. Vera idly wondered if this was the one who bit Roxanne at KidCare.

"New to BL?" she asked.

"Yeah," the woman said. "I mean, new to here. I was in Cincinnati before. Then off for a few years. Moved to Nashville, had the kid and my boyfriend split."

"Welcome to the ward," Vera said.

"Thanks."

"Hey kiddo!" Vera gave the boy her best grandma smile.

He frowned at her and stuck out his tongue. But at least he had stopped screaming.

"Do I have any points?" the woman asked.

"Three," Vera said.

The woman sighed. She took her groceries and left, the boy looking back after Vera and making faces.

Vera skimmed the woman's Index. She was working KidCare and retraining for nannying. That would be a tough sell with a kid, Vera thought. No rich families wanted BL kids tainting their sheltered little angels. Hopefully the woman had a relative who would watch the kid for free while she worked. Goodness knows nannying didn't pay enough to cover childcare.

Vera checked her own points balance. Her manager had given her a bonus for helping train some new workers on the registers. She normally got hers for being on time to work, for not missing any days, and for providing good service. You got more if you did retraining, but Vera was too old and tired for that. She felt lucky to sit on a stool all day.

Vera helped a few more of her Thursday customers. To keep the store from getting too crowded, everyone had a designated day for picking up their rations. You could come a different day, but you got points for coming when you were supposed to come.

Vera yawned and looked at the clock. Four hours left. Her manager came by and told her it was time for her break.

"Can I take it later?" she asked. "Bob was going to come by after work so we could have dinner together."

"Sure," he said. This guy was her favorite manager. He had a soft spot for the older ladies. He put another checker on break and went back to his office. He had grown up on BL and worked his way up. Now he rented a small apartment with his wife and children and took the bus back to the BL ward five days a week. Everyone in management was former BL.

Bob came in an hour later, carrying two dinner packs. The manager gave her permission to go and they went to the break room. Bob's hair was still wet from his shower. He got two cups of water from the faucet while she opened up the packs. She poured the water in and put the packs in the microwave. Algae substitute noodles, meatballs, and marinara. Bob refilled their waters. Vera got the salt and pepper shakers. That was a nice bonus of eating in the break room, because they didn't have to use their own salt and pepper rations.

Bob changed the TV channel to a reality show featuring BL lottery winners. It was in the middle of a segment on a new winner showing off his big house, sports car, designer clothes, and refrigerator full of food.

"Those people make us look bad," Bob said, gesturing with his fork. "If I won the lotto, you wouldn't see me living all crazy like that. I'd buy us into an Enclave. Nothing super fancy. Just a nice place for us to live the rest of our days."

"We could travel too," Vera said. "Maybe fly to Mexico or the Bahamas."

"We could do one trip. Maybe two." Bob said. "If there was enough after the Enclave. That's the most important thing. We would probably give some to Jolene. I think money concerns is what's keeping them from having babies."

"I would want to put some aside for Bob Jr.," Vera said. "Keep him off BL once he's out."

"It'll be nigh on impossible for him to get a job," Bob

said. "Giving him money won't fix that."

"I'd still want to give him something. It wouldn't be fair just to give Jolene some and not him."

"Alright, fine. We can give him something."

The second half of the show featured a winner who was back on BL only two years after leaving it. The host interviewed her in her small BL apartment as she complained about all the people who showed up looking for handouts. A boyfriend convinced her to invest in his business, which went bust. She was sued four times. She then tried to Peace Out, but the Facilitator referred her to a therapist. Now she was back to sewing at a BL clothing factory.

"See, in the regular lotto, you can be anonymous," Bob said. "It ain't like that with the BL lotto."

"Kind of fun to see their faces when they find out, though," Vera said.

Vera and Bob regularly watched the monthly BL lotto drawings. The drawing itself was done the night before the show aired, so that a crew could be sent to film the big winner, if any. If there wasn't one, then the money went into a jackpot for the next drawing.

A while back, nobody won for ten months straight. Vera thought about getting some tickets, but Bob did the math and decided it wasn't worth it. He claimed if there was no winner for twenty-three months, then the odds would be better and that's when they should get tickets. Vera never understood how he came to these conclusions.

"Break's over," she said, dumping their empty trays in the trash.

"See you at home," Bob said.

MARI AND VICTOR

The poor need to know they exist on sufferance. Their very lives are supported by the charity of individuals and the government. In other times and other places, they would simply be dead.
Post on the Bah!Humbug Tumblr, 3/21/2035.

"The big project for the semester is going to be your Index," Mr. Pao said. He wore a fitted white dress shirt with cufflinks and pale grey slacks. His shoes were shiny black leather and his wiry black hair was slicked back. "Testing starts in just a few months. Your scores and essays are going to be a major factor in whether you get sponsored."

Mari rolled her eyes. These new teachers, fresh out of college and cutting their teeth on a year in the BL ward. They knew nothing.

"Come on, Pao-man," Victor called from the back of the classroom. "Nobody gets sponsored."

"That's because nobody works on their Index," Mr. Pao said. "My goal is to get every single one of you a sponsor of some kind."

"Bullshit," Victor said.

Mr. Pao looked down at his tablet. "Victor Mendoza?"

"That's me."

"No cussing in my class."

"Fuck you," Victor said.

"OK, Victor," Mr. Pao replied. "If all you want in life is to skim algae pools until they Peace you Out, that is your choice. But I'm telling you there is another way. Hear me out or get out." Mr. Pao went to the classroom door and opened it. "Well?"

Victor sauntered toward the door. He stopped in front of Mr. Pao, put one hand on his shoulder and pushed him gently. "Nobody tells me what to do, hear that?" He pushed a little harder. "Nobody."

Pao's face remained calm. "Sit down or get out, Victor."

Mari held her breath, knowing Victor wouldn't back down in front of his friends. He was usually good at cowing the new teachers, but Pao was strangely unafraid.

"You wanna call security?" Victor asked. "Maybe you better. It takes them two minutes to get here. Wanna know what I can do in two minutes?"

"Sit down or get out," Pao repeated.

"Aw Pao-man, why you gotta be like this?" Victor shook his head sadly, drew back his fist and swung at Pao's head.

"Fight!" shouted one of the other boys. The kids jumped out of their desks to form a ring.

But it was already over. Pao had Victor face down on the ground, immobilized.

"He got the kung-fu!" shouted Jesse. "Bad ass motherfucking chino!"

Mari winced. Victor would make Jesse pay for that.

"No cussing in my class," Pao said calmly. "And for future reference, I am of Filipino descent."

"Yeah man, whatever," Jesse said.

"Victor, I'm going to let you up now," Mr. Pao said. "OK?"

"Yeah, Pao-man," Victor grunted.

Pao let go. Victor whipped his legs around, kicking at Pao's knees. Pao jumped back and used the heel of his shoe to stomp on Victor's ankle. Pao got him back on the floor, this time lifting Victor's arm so high Mari heard it pop. Victor groaned, his face pressed against the concrete.

The guard arrived thirty seconds later and took in the scene. "Mendoza again?" he said. "No surprise there."

"We had some differences over how I conduct my class." Pao looked down at Victor. "Brace yourself," he said. Pao rolled Victor onto his back, keeping a firm grip on his arm. He put his foot into Victor's armpit and pulled. Victor cried out, biting his lip so hard Mari could see a little drop of blood well at the corner of his mouth. "He'll need a sling," Pao told the guard. "And ice for his ankle."

"Get up, Mendoza," the guard ordered.

Victor got to his feet, cradling his arm and limping.

"See you tomorrow," Pao said. "I trust we understand each other now."

"You don't want him suspended?" the guard asked.

"I think he's been punished enough." Pao turned back to the class. "Take your seats, please."

They obeyed. Mari saw some of their friends exchange glances, deciding whether it was worth it to take on the bad ass mother-fucker.

"Where did you learn to fight like that?" Jesse asked.

"The ward in Hilo. I was on the MMA team in high

school."

"You were on BL?"

"Until I was 18," Mr. Pao said. "So now you know I'm one of you. I've been what you've been through. I've lived like you live. And I got out."

Mari raised her hand.

"Yes?"

"It don't matter, Mr. Pao. Victor's right about sponsors. Anybody does real good here and they go to the Keller Schools. They get the sponsors, not us. Why bother?"

Pao looked at his tablet. "Mari Ruiz?"

"Yeah."

"There are more than just college sponsors. There are companies out there who invest in BL kids. It's good PR. They have summer bridge programs to help you transition out. Your Index just has to show them you are ready. I didn't go to the Keller Schools. I got a corporate sponsor and scrubbed toilets in an office building for three years. I saved up and polished my Index. Took a few classes online and did well enough to convince someone to give me a student loan."

"Scrubbing toilets?" Mari asked.

"It's better than the algae pools," Mr. Pao said. "But there are other jobs. Assembly lines. Nannying."

"I'm not gonna be no nanny," Jesse scoffed.

"Probably not," Pao said with a hint of a smile. He looked at his tablet. "You did well in auto shop. Maybe you could put in for an apprenticeship with a mechanic."

"You're on bliss. None of us are gonna get sponsors."

"Only because of your own short-sightedness."

"Nothing about me is short, Pao-man." Jesse laughed.

Pao leaned back on his desk. "Most of you are what, second, third generation BL? Your moms only got off long enough to have you. You think this is the only possible life for you. And maybe for some of you, it is. You're too dumb or lazy or damaged or maybe some combination of all three."

The class erupted. "*Pendejo*," Jesse hissed.

Mari was pretty sure teachers weren't supposed to talk to them like that, but who knew? At least Pao was talking to them. Her history teacher had recorded all her lectures years ago and just played them for the class while she read books or dozed, snoring into her double chin. She had also given the same multiple-choice tests for twenty years, so anyone who gave a damn could find them and memorize the answers. Mari got a perfect score on the last test and couldn't even remember what it was about.

Pao reached into his desk drawer and took out an orange. He set it on his desk. The room went quiet. He took out another one. "How many of you have had an orange before?"

"We got half of one at Thanksgiving last year," Mari volunteered.

"What do you think it would be like, to be able to walk into a grocery store and buy real food? To wear clothes that aren't from the Don or BL issue?"

Mari knew what it was like. Her mom got them off BL for almost two years. In the beginning she came home each week with a new kind of fruit for them to try. One apple. One kiwi. One peach. A handful of cherries. Mari's favorite was the pineapple, even though it cut her tongue when she tried to eat the rind. Then her mom got knocked up. She claimed it was her boss and he would have to pay, but the DNA test proved her wrong. By that time it was too late to do anything but keep Baby Marcus, so they were back on BL. Not enough money doing hotel laundry to pay for someone to watch him. Marcus was four now. Mari had to pick him up from KidCare after school.

Mr. Pao peeled both oranges, broke them into segments and passed them out. He threw the peels in the trash.

"Think of this as a taste of what your life could be like," he said. "A life where you could have an orange every day if you wanted."

Mari pocketed hers. She would share it with Marcus when she got home. Jesse pocketed his too. Mari wondered how much bliss it would get him.

When the bell rang, Mari waited until the class cleared out. Mr. Pao was seated at his desk.

"Can I have the peels?" Mari asked.

"Just so you know, they aren't edible," Mr. Pao said.

"The orange part is," she replied. Mari ignored the pity in his eyes. "Can I have them or not?"

"Go ahead," Mr. Pao said.

Mari dug into the trash and put the peels in her bag.

Victor was waiting for her outside the classroom. His arm was supported by a strip of cloth and the scrape on his cheek had scabbed over. "What took you so long?"

"Nothing," she said. "You OK?"

"Yeah."

"I think Pao is for real."

"I don't know, *juera*."

"He's an asshole, but he's for real." Mari could tell she wasn't convincing Victor. She knew he was going to end up in juvie if he tried to take on Mr. Pao again. She reached into her bag and took out her orange segment. "He gave us these." She held it out to him. "I got an extra one for you."

"Liar," Victor said. "Put it back in your bag."

Mari obeyed.

"I know what you're trying to do," he said.

"You gonna give him a chance?"

"You want me to?"

"Yeah," Mari said. "Will you?"

"For you? Anything." Victor slung his arm around her and they went to their next class.

JEREMY AND RACHEL

It makes me proud to be an American. Proud that our country has declared that we will not allow our citizens to go hungry. We will not allow our citizens to be without homes. We will not deny our citizens access to the best healthcare in the world. Basic Living does this. Basic Living says something about America. That we have seen the evil in walking past our neighbor and leaving him beaten in the gutter. That we see it as our duty, nay, our moral obligation, to provide a path for our nation's tired, its poor, its tempest-tossed. To help them breathe free. God bless America!

President Williams, signing the Basic Living Act into law, 3/21/35.

Jeremy rushed over to the sleek black Lincoln as it pulled into the entryway. He waited for it to stop, then opened the rear door. A well-dressed elderly woman beamed at him.

"Good evening, Mrs. Thibodaux," he said, offering her his arm. She was one of his favorites. Knew the names of all the Enclave employees without having to read their name tags.

"Thank you, Jeremy," she said, stepping out of the car. Jeremy breathed through his mouth, trying to avoid the chemical odors wafting from her precisely curled white hair.

"How was dinner?" he asked.

"Would you believe Mr. Lawson took me to the Varsity for a chili burger and onion rings?" she drawled.

"Yes, ma'am."

"Best meal I've had in years."

"Yes, ma'am."

Mr. Lawson came around the back of the car. "I'll take over from here, Jeremy," he said.

"Yes, sir." Jeremy walked ahead of them and held open the door.

"You have a good evening, now," Mrs. Thibodaux said as they strolled past.

"Thank you, ma'am," Jeremy said. He went back to the valet stand and wiped the sweat from his forehead with a towel.

The passenger window of the Lincoln rolled down. "Get in," Tyler called from the driver's seat.

"I can't," Jeremy said. "I'm the only one on duty."

"It's air-conditioned."

"What if a car comes?"

"I'll see it in the rearview."

Jeremy went over to the window and leaned in. Icy air blasted against his face.

"Not too bad, right?" Tyler adjusted his black cap. It was his first day as a driver.

"Not bad at all," Jeremy said. "Are you done for the night?"

"Yeah," Tyler said. "It's past bedtime for most of the rezzies. Marty and Clara were getting all crazy staying out until ten."

"You like it better than the valet stand?"

"So far. Sure beats melting out there. Pays more, of course."

"Enough to move out of the bunkhouse?"

"Yeah. Shana wants to put in for a private room. Get married."

"Seriously? What kind of contract?"

"Permanent. She's not into that term option thing."

"You ready for that?"

"I think so, man." Tyler drummed on the steering wheel with both hands. "With my raise, we can do it. Save up to rent our own place in a year or two."

"You guys want babies?" Since children were not allowed in employee housing, the only reason to move out was to start a family. Jeremy couldn't imagine it. Tyler was only a few years older than Jeremy, twenty-three tops.

"Just one," Tyler said. "Any more and we'll be back on Basic Living."

"What's the rush?"

"We've been together since junior high," Tyler said. "What's your problem?"

"Nothing. I'm happy for you, man. I really am."

"Whatever," Tyler said. He looked in the rearview. "Car coming."

It was Mr. Grier's brand new screaming red convertible. He was passed out in the passenger seat. The car pulled to the curb and stopped. "You have arrived," chirped a female voice with a British accent. Mr. Grier didn't move.

"Drunk again?" Tyler asked.

"Looks like it," Jeremy said. "At least he didn't throw up this time."

"You got this?"

"I got it. We OK?"

"Sure, man. I know you're just looking out." Tyler checked the time. "I'm gonna park and see what Shana's doing." The black Lincoln pulled around the corner and into the Enclave's underground parking lot.

Jeremy called the front desk and scanned Mr. Grier's thumb. The old man's head lolled to the side and he started snoring. Jeremy watched drool seep into his collar.

A few minutes later, a heavyset nurse came out with a wheelchair. She was wearing orthotic shoes and pink scrubs with a print of calico cats. She checked Mr. Grier's pulse and took a quick blood alcohol level. She sighed. "Can you help me transfer him?"

"Sure," Jeremy said. He hauled Mr. Grier over one shoulder and lowered him into the wheelchair.

"Thanks." The nurse crouched down and fastened the straps. "This idiot is going to drink himself to death. Maybe I won't give him a saline bag." Catching Jeremy's quizzical look, she explained. "Without the saline drip he'll have one nasty hangover."

"Can you actually do that?"

"I wish," she said. "The most I can do is recommend counseling. Like he'd take it."

"Can you really blame him? His wife just died."

"There are other ways to handle grief." The nurse tightened the straps and heaved herself up. Jeremy held the door for her while she wheeled Mr. Grier in.

Jeremy slid into the red convertible and parked it in Mr. Grier's spot. A lot of the rezzies used Enclave drivers, especially since there was such a long wait-list for parking spots. Mr. Grier had switched out his Bentley for the convertible a week after his wife Peaced Out. Jeremy often wondered what people had done before they retired, to be able to afford a place like this. The rezzies didn't talk much with the staff though. Most didn't even bother to read his name tag.

In training, they learned how to be deferential and polite. How to speak in a more refined manner. The rezzies didn't want to hear any BL slang. Getting valet was actually a pretty good placement. Jeremy worked hard at it. He memorized all the rezzies' names so he could greet them properly. His manager noticed that and made him head valet whenever he was on day shift, even though other guys had more seniority. It gave him a little extra cash, which he used to take online classes at Marietta Community College. Right now he was just learning all the stuff he should have learned in high school, but he hoped to get a college sponsor. Maybe someday he would have his own red convertible, just like Mr. Grier.

But first he would get his mom and sister off BL. Find a place with room for all of them. Jeremy thought about that a lot.

Every month he took the bus back to the ward to visit them, bringing fresh fruit and vegetables in his backpack. His mom worked at the elementary school cafeteria where his sister was in fourth grade. His father had died the week after Rachel was born.

Jeremy's family had bounced on and off BL for years. His dad had trouble holding down a job. Jeremy was ten when his dad finally found work that suited him. He drove big trucks across the country, hauling tomatoes or grapes or whatever for a week or two at a time. Once he got promoted to solo gigs, Jeremy's mom pushed to have one more baby. Try for a little girl. His dad agreed. After a few days off with his new baby, he went on the road with a load of cucumbers and never came back. The accident was blamed on heavy fog.

Jeremy's mom tried to keep them off BL, but with a new baby it was impossible. The trucking company covered funeral expenses, but they had never been much for saving. So BL was the only life Rachel knew. They still went to their old church, though. The deacons made sure they had bus vouchers so they could attend.

At nine years old, Rachel was finally beginning to understand the difference between her and the other little girls at church. Rachel was the one who got their old clothes and shoes, discreetly handed to her mother in garbage bags at the end of service. Then she got to hear about the girls' shopping trips for back-to-school clothes or a Christmas outfit or a birthday dress. A few months ago, Rachel had taken him through her closet and told him about the prior owner of each of her threadbare Sunday dresses. He was already saving up to buy her a brand new dress.

Rachel was always invited to the girls' birthday parties, but she rarely got to go unless the parents were willing to pick her up and drop her off. When that happened, she used up her points to get a present at the Don. For the most part, the birthday girls were getting better at pretending to be happy with the used book or shabby toy wrapped in plain paper.

Rachel loved to talk about the girls' bedrooms, closets packed to the brim with colorful clothes, fluffy comforters on princess beds with canopies. Dollhouses as tall as she was. But her favorite part was the cake and ice cream. That was something they never got to have on BL.

On Jeremy's last visit, Rachel had confided that the pastor's daughter said she only invited Rachel to her birthday party because she was supposed to be nice to poor people. It was something Rachel would never have told their mother and she begged Jeremy not to tell the pastor. Jeremy promised to keep it a secret, but for a moment he enjoyed the thought of smacking the pastor's daughter across her plump and piggish face.

Jeremy went back to the valet stand and shut it down for the night. Since it was so late, he was allowed to use the lobby elevator to get down to the bunkhouse. The crystal chandeliers were dimmed and two janitors were vacuuming and wiping down the furniture. Jeremy waved at them, then took the elevator down to sub-level 3. He went straight to the showers, tossing his uniform into the laundry bin and grabbing a fresh towel.

Afterward, he went back to the room he shared with five other guys, including Tyler. The door had no lock, but each of them had a secure locker. Jeremy pressed his thumb against the scanner and the locker popped open. He got dressed and took out his phone. He had three missed calls, a voicemail from his mother and a text from Tyler, telling him to meet them in the staff room. It was big enough for meetings and in the evenings employees were allowed to use it as a place to hang out. Over the years, discarded furniture and rugs from the upper levels made their way down. It was a pretty cozy spot.

Jeremy checked his message first.

"It's Mom. Call me as soon as you get this." She sounded as if she had been crying. "It doesn't matter what time it is. It's about Rachel."

Jeremy quickly called her back. She picked up on the first ring.

"What's wrong, Mom. Is Rachel OK?"

"No," his mother said, her voice catching. "She is not OK."

"What happened? Where is she?"

"She's in the hospital. It's cancer."

"What are you talking about?" Jeremy said incredulously. "She can't have cancer."

"It's a brain tumor. Remember last year how she was saying she couldn't see so well and we took her in to get glasses? They think it was the tumor."

"How do they know? Maybe they're wrong."

"They showed me on the scan, Jeremy. She fainted during recess today. They couldn't get her to wake up for hours."

"Is she in surgery? Are they doing chemo? What's going on?"

"They aren't doing anything." His mother broke down, her voice thick with pain.

"Why?" Jeremy asked, a cold feeling spreading through his stomach. "Why aren't they doing anything?"

"The doctor said the cancer is too big to operate and her chances of survival are less than fifty percent. Basic Living won't cover it. They'll only cover pain meds until she... They said I could take her to Peace Out when it gets bad."

"They have to treat her!" Jeremy said. "How much does it cost if we pay for it?"

Jeremy's mother just cried into the phone.

"How much do they want?" Jeremy demanded, trying to keep his voice calm.

"Thirty thousand," his mother choked. "That's just for the chemo. A lot more for the surgery. I didn't ask how much."

"Did you talk to someone at church?"

"I did," she said. "I called Deacon Jennings. He wanted the doctor's phone number."

"Did he call you back?"

"This afternoon. He said thirty thousand is their entire

mercy budget for the year and her prognosis is very bad. They won't help. He said they will pray for her." His mother's voice was bitter.

"What about asking people at church for donations?"

"He says people at church don't have a lot of money to give and it would be better spent elsewhere." His mother resumed crying.

"I'll get the money."

"How?" his mother sobbed.

"Don't worry. I'll figure it out."

HENRY

"I see it all the time. I get patients in and they are wearing new Nikes and Ralph Lauren shirts. Then I open their file and see they are on Medicaid and welfare. I can't even afford to buy those kinds of clothes for my own kids. The key is that money is fungible. You give those people money and they spend it on drugs, alcohol, cigarettes, televisions and clothes. Then they go looking for handouts at food banks, churches, and homeless shelters. Basic Living will put a stop to all that. They'll get rations for everything. I can walk by panhandlers without guilt, knowing that they just need to go to a BL store to get food or shoes, or to a BL complex to get housing. So yeah, my senator better vote for this, or I know I'll be voting for someone else come November."

Word on the Street, ABC, Interview with Nancy Mueller, Pediatrician, New Orleans, LA, 10/12/34.

Over a week had passed since Henry gave Mike his drawing. So far, nothing bad had happened. That first night, Henry hardly slept. He thought about trying to hide the rest of his drawings, but where? Not the utility shed on the roof. Mr.

Bautista worked there all the time. They wouldn't be safe at school either. A janitor might find them and throw them away. Henry had begged his mom to keep his stuff safe and she promised. He knew though. He knew if Mike came back with a baggie of bliss, she'd hand over everything. So he left every morning with a twist of fear in his gut. A twist that only eased when he came home in the evening and confirmed that everything was intact.

Henry was finally starting to relax. Mr. Bautista's painting was done, and his wife had given him a can of sliced peaches as a thank you. Mr. Bautista said he didn't even have to give him candy bars anymore. That he should save his points for art supplies instead and that he could use their walls whenever he wanted. Those hours in the Bautista apartment had been surreal. The afternoon light streaming through the windows, his box of paints on the floor. Henry marked out the dimensions of his painting with some masking tape Mr. Bautista gave him and used an old toothbrush, dried out markers, and his fingers as improvised paintbrushes. He lost time. Each night Mr. Bautista had to stop him and send him home so they could go to bed.

Henry had used up all his paint. He was glad it was Tuesday so he could start collecting more. Henry looked at the clock on the wall of his classroom. Ten minutes until the final bell. His teacher was droning on about adding fractions when the door opened and the principal came in.

"Sorry to interrupt, Mrs. Morales," she said. "I need to speak with Henry."

"Go ahead, Henry," Mrs. Morales said.

Henry stood up slowly and packed his backpack, each movement controlled and casual while his mind raced through the possibilities. It had to be his mother. Had she overdosed on bliss? Had she missed work? Had she shown up high and made a big mistake? Were they finally sending her to Sanctuary? Had she been beat up bad enough to go to the clinic? Henry thought Mike had put a stop to that part of it. Each step he took toward the principal felt a little more like death.

"Hurry up, Henry," his teacher said.

Henry did not look at the faces of his classmates. There was nothing to be seen there. There would be no commiseration. No sympathy. Not for invisible Henry. He followed the principal out the door.

"My mom," he whispered.

"What was that?"

"My mom," he said, a little louder. "What happened to her?"

"What?" the principal looked confused for a moment. "Ah. Don't worry, Henry. Your mother is just fine. In fact, she is in the office waiting for you. This is about you."

"I don't understand."

"You'll see in just a minute." The principal led him to her office and opened the door. "Go on in."

Henry saw his mother, Mike, and an older woman he didn't recognize. A rich woman, judging by her jewelry and clothes.

"Have a seat, Henry," the principal said.

As Henry sat down, he saw a stack of paper on the desk. His drawings.

"I promise I didn't steal anything," he said. "I got it all from the trash. Everything."

"They know you didn't steal nothing, Henry," his mother said. "This is about your talent. Mike had the idea. We been working on it all week, taking your drawings to the principal here and she making calls. Mr. Bautista showed us what you done at his place too. Mike took a picture."

"I don't understand," Henry said.

"My name is Ms. Keller," said the woman he didn't recognize. "I direct the Keller Arts School in New York. I'm here to offer you a place in our freshman class."

"No," Henry said.

"Do you know much about the Keller Schools and what we do?" she asked.

Henry shook his head.

"The first school was founded by my father almost forty years ago. He strongly believed there were many children on BL with potential that wasn't being realized. So he gathered the best minds in education, bought a building just outside Seattle, and started the first Keller School. The school was a great success and he was able to open seven additional schools across the country. Over the years, we have helped thousands of bright young people find success. We want to help you do the same."

"Henry, this is a wonderful opportunity," his principal coaxed. "In all my years here, only five other students have qualified to go to a Keller School."

"If I go, I have to live there," Henry said flatly.

"That's true," Ms. Keller said. "We find that our students do best when taken out of the Basic Living environment. You board with us year-round, but we'll provide a travel voucher to your mom so she can visit one Saturday each month. It's only a three hour train ride from here. As an art student, you would also go to different camps for part of the summer. We hold an institute in Paris every August."

"You hear that, Henry?" Mike said. "You hit the big time."

"Thanks for the offer," Henry said. "No."

"I understand," Ms. Keller said. "I'm asking you to leave behind your friends and family and that's difficult. But you have an amazing talent, Henry. What you've managed to do with scraps of paper and broken crayons is nothing short of a miracle. At the school, we'll be able to give you paint, canvas, brushes. Whatever medium you want to work in. You will have teachers to help you grow as an artist. When you graduate, you will have any number of colleges vying for your attendance."

"It's a way out, Henry," his mom said. "This is your chance."

"I don't want to leave you," Henry said. "You need me."

"I'll take care of your mom," Mike said. "You don't have to worry."

"Why are you doing this?" Henry demanded. "What's in it for you?"

"Just trying to help you out, boy."

"Yeah, right."

Mike bristled at that.

"You don't have to decide today," Ms. Keller said calmly, looking back and forth between them. "You don't even have to decide this week or this month. We'll take you when you are ready. If you change your mind, I'm heading back to New York in the morning. The train leaves at ten and I have an extra ticket."

"This is how it's gonna go, Henry," Mike said. "You gonna go to that Keller School. You gonna work your ass off. You gonna get yourself famous. Then you gonna get your momma and me off BL. Set us up real nice so she don't have to *work* no more. You get my meaning?"

"I get it," Henry said. His mom was in the bathroom,

probably dropping a little bliss to get her through the night.

"Don't you want that for her? Don't you care about your momma?"

"Do you?"

"I sure do, boy."

"Then I want her to stop *working* now. I'll go if you can do that. Can you keep her in bliss without her having to *work*?"

"She got a habit, Henry. It ain't cheap."

"It would be cheaper if you didn't take a cut."

"Someone has to protect her," Mike said. "Who's that gonna be? You?"

"I'm not leaving her."

"Then I guess I don't need to protect her anymore," Mike said. "I wonder how they'll treat her when they know they don't gotta answer to Big Mike for any damage to the goods." Big Mike was his fighting name. He was six feet four and 230 pounds of powerful muscle.

Henry's mother had taken him to see a fight once. Mike had worn nothing but a pair of shiny boxing shorts, his oiled torso glistening under the lights. Big Mike was the headliner, the last fight of the night. Henry hated the way Mike toyed with his opponent, a fighter brought in from the ward in San Diego. The crowd loved it, egging him on. Mike finally decided to put an end to it and bashed the guy on the side of the head. The guy staggered back with blood dripping down his ear, everybody roaring. Mike slammed him onto the mat, jamming his forearm against the guy's neck. The fighter tapped out and Mike was declared the winner. He won a thousand points that night.

Before Mike, Henry's mother had been beaten up pretty regularly. A black eye one evening, bruises on her back another. The same guy, coming back for more and his mother not turning him away, her need for bliss winning. It was what got Henry in trouble. He had been eleven when he tracked the man down to a building on the other side of the ward. Henry brought a wrench he had stolen from Mr. Bautista's toolbox and waited outside the man's building. When he saw the man come out, Henry attacked. But the man easily disarmed Henry and was using the wrench to work him over when a deep voice said, "Leave the kid alone."

The man had immediately stopped, but protested. "Mike, this kid's just getting what's coming to him." He showed Mike the bloody welt on the back of his neck.

"Why would you do that, kid?"

Henry blinked blood out of his eyes. A large man stood over him. Shaved head. Sunglasses.

"Answer me, boy."

"My momma," Henry stammered. "He hurt my momma."

"She ain't one of yours," the man interjected.

Mike ignored him. "This is a beautiful boy," he had said, almost to himself. "I wonder if your momma is beautiful, too?" Mike had taken Henry back to his apartment and patched him up. Then he drove Henry home in one of the BL construction pick-up trucks. Mike took to Henry's mother right away and she to him. Three years later and Mike still came to their house every few days to see her. She hadn't been beaten up since.

"You wouldn't let anyone hurt her," Henry said. "I don't believe you."

"I got a dozen girls younger and prettier," Mike said. "I got a fondness for your momma, that's true. But that don't change anything. You're going to that school."

"Then she stops *working*."

"I can't promise that, Henry."

"All my old drawings. You can have them. Even now they're worth something, right? And if I get famous they'll be worth a lot."

"Your momma was going to give me those anyway in thanks for my help."

"They aren't hers. If I go tell that Keller lady you trying to steal my stuff, what she gonna to do to you? She got money and that savior thing those rich white people got. She'd scoop Mom and me right outta here to protect us. But you promise and I'll give them to you straight up. Write it down so I can't change it later."

"I want ten percent of your earnings too."

"I haven't earned anything."

"You will. Those Keller folk make sure you all successful. Makes them look good."

"All my old drawings. Ten percent of whatever I make. And my mom stops *working*. Now."

"Deal," Mike said. "Write it down."

"Write what down?" his mom asked, shutting the bathroom door behind her.

"Just a little agreement I made with Henry," Mike said. "He's decided to go to New York in the morning."

"I'm proud of you, baby," his mom said dreamily. "I'm gonna miss you, but I'm so proud of you."

After buying Henry a bagel and hot chocolate, Ms. Keller worked for the whole train ride. She gave him a sketch pad, a pack of colored pencils, and a pencil sharpener to keep him occupied. At lunchtime they ate in the dining car while she took calls. Henry didn't know what to order, so he let Ms. Keller do it for him. She ordered lemonade, a turkey sandwich with side of fruit salad, and a chocolate chip cookie. He had never tasted anything so good. It was way better than that can of peaches the Bautistas gave him.

At the train station in New York, a car was waiting for them. Ms. Keller told the driver to take them to the nearest Target. Henry had never been inside a regular store before. It was enormous. Gleaming. Shiny. Full of people pushing carts of stuff he never knew he needed. He looked down at his BL issue clothes and felt out of place.

"What are we doing here?" Henry asked.

"We're here to get you a new wardrobe," Ms. Keller said. She led him to the boys section. "You're probably a 12 in pants. Maybe a medium in shirts." She started pulling clothes off the racks. "If you see anything you like, put it in the cart."

Henry's backpack contained all his worldly possessions. His art book. Three pairs of underwear. One more pair of pants. Two shirts. All BL issue. He could have used his points on clothes at the Don. Some of the kids were really into that, but he had never cared about clothes.

"Nothing?" Ms. Keller asked.

"I got clothes," Henry said. "You don't gotta buy me clothes."

"I don't have to buy you clothes," Ms. Keller corrected. "Your clothes identify you as a recipient of Basic Living. As a student at the Keller Schools, we train you for a life off of Basic Living. You should dress accordingly."

"I'll pay you back."

"This isn't my money, Henry," Ms. Keller said. "It belongs to the school and there is a fund for this purpose."

"I'll still pay it back."

"I hope you will," Ms. Keller said. "Almost all of our alumni make generous donations." He followed her to the changing rooms. "Try them on and come out so I can see."

Henry modeled a half dozen pairs of pants and a dozen shirts. Ms. Keller was pleased to see she had guessed right about his sizes. She disappeared and came back with more clothes. "Try these on too."

He complied. When he finished she told him to get dressed and bring out the clothes. He dumped them back into the cart.

"Let's see," she said. "We'll need socks, underwear, and shoes too. And a coat. What else?" She wheeled the cart around for another pass through the boy's section.

At the end of the visit, Henry found himself the owner of three pairs of jeans, one pair of black pants and two pairs of khakis. He had four button-down shirts, three long-sleeved t-shirts, five short-sleeved t-shirts, a hoodie and a sweater. He had a coat. Two pairs of pajamas. A dozen pairs of socks. A swim suit. Eight pairs of boxers. Tennis shoes. Boots. Flip flops. She also bought him a small suitcase. For summer camp, she explained.

At the checkout stand, she pressed her thumb to the pad without checking the total. Henry looked. One thousand eight hundred sixty-four dollars and seventy-two cents.

"It's too much," he blurted.

"It's the bare minimum," Ms. Keller said firmly. She picked out a set of clothes and handed them to him. "Take the tags off and go change."

Henry did as he was told.

"Much better," Ms. Keller said when he returned, taking his old clothes and dropping them into the trash. "Let's go." When she walked ahead of him, Henry got his BL clothes out of the trash and put them in his backpack.

The car idled in front of Target. The driver got out to load Henry's new stuff into the trunk then dropped them off at a building in Greenwich Village. Ms. Keller was greeted inside by a frazzled young woman in a suit. "You're late for your three o'clock," she said. "I've got Barry in there."

"Barry is perfectly capable of handling Mr. Yamashiro," Ms. Keller said. "Could you please take Henry to his room? His roommate will be done with class soon. Henry, your roommate's name is Scott. He's going to show you the ropes." She gave Henry a brief pat on the arm. "I'm glad you chose to come." She headed for the stairs.

"I'm Ms. Keller's assistant," the young woman said. "You need help with those bags?"

"I got it," Henry said.

Henry's dorm room was the same size as the studio he had shared with his mother. He had a lofted bed with a desk and chair underneath. The dresser was next to the bed. There was one closet with ten empty blue hangers. The bedding was navy blue plaid and Henry figured that the blue towels in the bathroom were his too. His roommate's stuff was green. Henry took all the tags off his clothes and put them away. He hid his BL clothes in the back of the bottom drawer. The desk was stocked with school supplies and there was an envelope in his chair. Henry took out a thin, flexible sheet of plastic. A sticky note was attached, welcoming him to the Keller Arts School.

"Hey," a voice said from the doorway. "You must be Henry. I'm Scott." Scott was a white boy. Skinny but almost as tall as Henry.

"Hey," Henry said. "What's this?" He held up the sheet.

"It's your tablet." Scott dropped his backpack on the desk and plopped down in his chair. He swiveled to face Henry. "State of the art. Full Internet access. Nothing like those clunky BL issues."

Henry touched the face of the plastic and it lit up. "Cool," he said.

"So what are you in for? You must be pretty awesome if Keller Herself went to get you."

"I draw." It sounded strange to say it out loud.

"That's cool. My old roommate was an artist too."

"What happened to him?" Henry asked.

"His parents got off BL." Scott shrugged. "It happens a lot. We get a lot of kids who are only here a year or two."

"How long have you been here?"

"Three years. My mom is almost done with her degree though."

"What are you in for?" Henry asked, mimicking Scott's slang.

"I sing. Musical theater. I was an academic admission too though, once we were off short-term BL. This is the closest school to my mom. You're a freshman, right?"

"Yeah," Henry said.

"Gay or straight?"

"What?"

"Everyone likes to know. It's an art school. A sophomore girl already called dibs on you, if you're interested. She saw you come in. She's pretty cute. So are you gay or straight?"

"Straight." Henry eyed Scott. "You?"

"Straight." Scott laughed. "Don't worry, my girlfriend will vouch for me. You'll meet her at dinner. Are you ready for the grand tour?"

"Sure," Henry said, following Scott out the door.

"Your tablet has your class schedule and a map of the building," Scott said. "I'm guessing we are in a lot of the same classes. Our resident advisor is Thad. He lives at the end of the hall and is kind of like our big brother. He graduated from here a few years ago. He's studying film at NYU. Super laid back. You can have girls over whenever, and he doesn't care what you do so long as you're in the building by curfew. A few of the single faculty live in the dorms, too. Free rent in New York, so why not?" Scott knocked on Thad's door and waited. Nobody answered. "I bet he's in class right now, but he'll probably come by tonight. I'm sure Keller Herself has alerted him to your presence."

Scott took Henry to the elevator and pressed the down button. "We also have Dean Miranda. She's kind of like the replacement mom. She's really great to talk to if you have a problem or want some candy. She keeps a big jar on her desk. She's on vacation this week, but she'll definitely want to meet you when she gets back. She likes to have one on one time with each of us."

"Where are we going now?" Henry asked as they got on the elevator.

"The sixth floor," Scott said. "That's where a lot of our classes will be. This building is huge. The top five floors are dorms. The five below that are classrooms. Then it's the cafeteria and the gym, then the offices. You have to thumb in and out of the building so they can keep track of you. That's how you get in our room, too. Curfew is nine o'clock until you're sixteen, by the way. Then it's eleven."

When they got off the elevator, the hallway was bustling with students.

"Who is this?" a girl asked, walking up to them and linking her arm with Scott's.

"This is my new roomie, Henry. He's the artist from D.C. that Keller Herself recruited," Scott said. "Henry, meet my girlfriend Breann."

"Hi," Henry said awkwardly.

"Oh, he's shy!" Breann said, laughing. "And so cute."

Henry flushed.

"If Francine thinks she can just call dibs, she is absolutely wrong," Breann said. "I bet Talia pulls rank on her. Henry's just her type."

"Who's this, Breann?" Another girl joined their group. She wore a black leotard and legwarmers, her backpack slung over one shoulder. She gave Henry a thorough inspection.

"This is Henry," Breann said. "He's straight and an artist."

"I'm Emiko," the girl said. "It's nice to meet you. Want to take me for coffee later?"

"Uh," said Henry.

"Give the poor guy a break," Scott said. "He got here twenty minutes ago. Let me finish showing him around, OK ladies?"

Breann kissed Scott goodbye and walked off with Emiko, who turned back to wink at Henry.

"Don't worry," Scott assured him. "You have the right to refuse any and all advances."

"I'm not used to it," Henry said. "Back home I was the weird kid nobody talked to…"

"This whole school is the weird kids!" Scott declared. "You're going to fit right in." Scott showed Henry around the classrooms, then took him down to the cafeteria. Henry was astonished by the baskets of fruit on each table and the long buffet line, with a crew of cooks prepping vegetables and stirring steaming pots.

"Your first semester here, you'll be on the meal plan," Scott said. "You thumb in and out of the cafeteria and can eat whatever you want. You gotta learn portion control or you'll blow up." He puffed out his cheeks and held out his arms. "If you gain more than ten pounds, you get sent to the nutritionist." He picked up an apple and tossed it to Henry. He selected another one for himself.

As Scott showed Henry around the building, Henry found himself shaking hands with dozens of people. Scott seemed so comfortable with everyone, it made Henry feel comfortable too.

"Anyway," Scott continued, "once you've passed the life skills test, they'll let you reduce your meal plan and you get money on your Index every month. So now I do breakfast and dinner at the cafeteria, but have lunch off campus with my friends."

"What if you run out?"

"Well, you're supposed to learn to budget, so you shouldn't run out. But if you do, then you bum off friends or don't eat. This one time, a girl used her whole month of money in one weekend. I heard Keller Herself let the girl starve for two days and then gave her AlgiProtein bars for the rest of the month. Lesson learned."

"Do I have to use the money on food for me? Could I use it to get my mom some vouchers?"

"You could, I guess. But why?"

"Dude, that's cold," Henry said. "You're living large and you can't help out your family?"

"They already get help," Scott said, surprised. "That's part of the deal when you come here. It's how my mom is going to college."

"Are you serious?"

"Yeah. You didn't know?"

"No," Henry said. But Mike knew, he thought. Mike knew exactly what he was doing.

"I bet your mom didn't want you to feel like she was

selling you," Scott said awkwardly. "My mom tried to refuse the stipend because she didn't want me to feel that way. But I told her she had to use it to go to school like me, and then it would be fair."

"My mom's boyfriend is the one who got me in here," Henry said. "He probably worked it out so he gets half her stipend even though he isn't my dad."

"Fuck him," Scott said. "You tell Keller Herself. She'll fix it."

"Nah," Henry said. "Mike and I have a deal. The stipend will help him hold up his end of it."

Henry could tell Scott wanted to know more, but was glad when he didn't probe. They were finally back at their dorm room.

"I have some homework to do before dinner," Scott said, taking out his tablet. "You have any questions?"

"Not right now," Henry said. He took out his tablet, too. After setting his password and sending an email to his mother, Henry looked up. "Hey Scott?"

"Yeah?"

"Thanks for being so nice to me."

"Sure," Scott replied. "We BL kids gotta stick together."

VERA AND BOB

After pirates hijacked a dozen barges carrying foodstuffs to the United States last week, the President today announced the deployment of thirty ships and submarines to the Pacific to serve as escorts.

The National Guard has been called upon to provide additional security at grocery stores across the nation after the riots in Los Angeles, Houston, Dallas, and Charlotte. Sales of seeds, fertilizer, and hydroponic equipment have quintupled, and so-called doomsday preppers are guarding their compounds day and night. Jedediah Buskirk, the spokesman at the largest known compound in Idaho, gave a statement.

"For years we have been considered an oddity. The delusional preppers hoarding food and weapons. Well, my friends, the skinny cows have devoured the fat cows. Judgment day is at hand and we will survive. Now get off my property." When this reporter failed to comply quickly, Buskirk aimed his semi-automatic rifle at the sky and fired several warning shots.

Joseph Partridge, President and Prophet of the Church of Latter Day Saints, issued a press release offering post-service meals on Sundays at all Mormon chapels. It is unclear how many meals will be served each Sunday or how long the offer will last. The Mormon church is known for requiring its members to store a year's supply of food, and it appears that the church itself has significant stockpiles of canned goods.

President Acosta's response to the world famine has been measured. She addressed the nation on Thursday. "We ask that the people of the United States remain calm. Ours is still a nation of plenty. A nation of innovation. A nation of solutions."

One corporation has emerged as the frontrunner in the government's search for alternate food sources. AlgiPro, a small start-up headquartered in Davis, California, has patented a series of genetically engineered algalbacterial symbionts. These symbionts consume almost any form of organic matter, producing a nutrient and protein dense algae.

According to AlgiPro's website, "AlgiPro is an incredibly versatile product. It can be mixed with spices and flavorings and compressed into bars. It can be dried, powdered and used as a substitute for flour. It can be processed into a meat substitute. AlgiPro, a proprietary blend of numerous algae strains, contains an optimal balance of carbohydrates, protein, and fat while also providing all essential amino acids, vitamins, and minerals."

The President declined to answer questions regarding rumors of the government's alleged negotiations with AlgiPro.

Worldwide Famine Enters Second Year, Reuters, 4/13/2025.

Vera had been surprised by the smell of the algae pools. She thought they would have reeked with the stench of raw sewage, but there was only a mild earthy odor that strengthened when the wind blew. Each pool was circular, two feet deep and a hundred feet in diameter. One long arm spanned the pool and slowly spun around a center axis, skimming algae from the surface. Two workers manned each pool, using tools with claw grabbers to move inorganics into the bins they wore at each hip. The motion of the skimmer directed algae to the center axis, where it was piped to the next processing stage.

The workers periodically emptied their bins into a large tub. At the end of each day this tub was taken to the recycling facility, where the trash was sorted by another set of workers. The algae was thick and slimy and the workers had to clear any clogs along the skimming arm and center axis.

Vera waved at the workers as she walked by. They wore waist-high waders, goggles and gloves up to their elbows, trudging through the pools in four two-hour shifts with twenty minute breaks in between. Cameras were mounted by each pool. Skimming was work for the young or troublesome. Managers monitored video feed from a windowless office in the processing plant. They had the power to issue warnings to workers for failure to work. Three warnings with video evidence meant a month-long trip to prison.

As Vera knew from Bob Jr., work in prison was the same with no breaks. The prison just outside Nashville had the largest AlgiPro plant in the state. Prisoners had to relieve themselves in the pools and got ten minutes at lunch to down one AlgiProtein bar and a pouch of water. Bob Jr. said that any guy who refused to work would just disappear. He didn't know where they went, but they were all lifers with no chance of parole. He figured they just didn't care what happened to them anymore. Vera figured they got Peaced Out.

The algae pools drained into a series of bioreactors below ground, each housing a different kind of algae. Vera had heard that the guys who cleaned the reactors had to wear full-body suits. Some of the more potent algae would eat through bare skin in minutes. Vera was happy Bob was old enough to have an easier job at the recycling facility. He sat on a bench all day and sorted plastics, glass, and metal onto different conveyer belts. The algae devoured any food left in the containers and scoured them clean of paper and glue. He was on day shift for the month and Vera liked to join him for lunch when she wasn't working.

It was nice to live close enough to walk to the facility. Bob told her that some of the workers were brought in from wards an hour away or more. Doing that commute every day would be awful, Vera thought as she took their BL packs to the lunch room. Vera stood by the windows overlooking the factory floor and spotted Bob at a conveyer belt in the middle of the enormous warehouse. He wasn't facing her, but she recognized the pattern of wispy salt and pepper hair on the back of his head. A bell sounded, and a third of the workers got up off their benches and shuffled toward the stairs. Bob was one of them. Vera got lunch ready and found a little table for the two of them. When Bob walked through the door, she signaled to get his attention.

"What do we have today?" he asked, sitting down.

"Sandwiches," she said.

"Do we have any ketchup left?"

"Used the last of it last night with dinner."

"That's too bad," Bob said.

"We'll get some more at McDonald's next week," Vera assured him. She was turning seventy.

"Did Jolene send the bus vouchers?"

"She's coming to pick us up herself!" Vera was excited to share the news. Jolene had called that morning with a change of plan. "Afterward, we're going to her house for the rest of the day. She's making a steak dinner!"

"With mashed potatoes and gravy?"

"She's using my old recipe, just the way you like it. Plus asparagus and a chocolate layer cake for dessert."

"Chris is letting her do all that?"

"She says it was his idea!"

"I don't quite believe that, but I'll take it," Bob said. He tore a piece of crust off his pale green sandwich and dunked it in his cup of water until it was soft enough to eat.

Jolene was right on time, picking them up outside their apartment complex. Her compact car was coated with a black solar paint that glittered in the late morning sun. Bob sat in the backseat, letting Vera ride in front since she got carsick. They were wearing some of the clothes they had before BL. The BL issue greys drew unwanted attention outside the wards. Bob's pale blue button-down shirt and slacks were a little loose on him these days, but his belt held things up. He had lost about twenty pounds after so many years on the BL diet. It was very nutritious. Everyone agreed on that. Periodic outings to McDonald's and the ketchup packets they hoarded didn't seem to make a difference.

Vera was in a simple lavender dress that fit nicely even though she too had lost weight. One of her friends worked at the sewing factory and had offered to alter it in exchange for another of Vera's old dresses. Over the years, Vera had traded away much of her clothing, but she kept a few things. She still had her wedding dress in a large white box. Jolene had worn it at her wedding and Vera hoped to have a granddaughter who would wear it someday. Jolene was looking good, Vera thought. Fit. She didn't look like she was thirty-six. That was how old Vera had been when Charlie was born. Vera hoped Jolene and Chris didn't wait much longer. It wasn't like they could afford fertility treatments. It seemed like the one thing scientists hadn't been able to change was the ticking of a woman's biological clock.

Vera thought she looked good too, for a woman her age. Before going on BL, Vera had been rather plump. She tried all sorts of diets, but never stuck to any of them long enough to lose much weight. Pocket change became candy bars, sodas, and chips in the vending machines at work. She found comfort in baking cakes, cookies, and brownies. Besides, Bob used to get grumpy when there were no desserts in the house. BL put a stop to all that.

Vera had seen a commercial for a high end AlgiPro diet. Bars, shakes, and powders made with only the best organically fed algae. They touted the use of green waste from farms across the country. Chaff from wheat grown in Iowa. Grape skins and stems from vineyards in California. Corn stalks, husks, and cobs from farms in Nebraska. And here everyone on BL got the diet for free. Of course, Vera thought, their algae was fed with the collected waste of the greater Nashville metropolis.

Vera once read a biography of the founder of AlgiPro, back when she had the energy to read. Shane Grier made a historic deal with the President during the Great Famine, followed by an accord with the United Nations. Algae pools and bioreactors were set up next to sewage processing plants and dumps all over the world. Back then nobody cared if their algae was grain fed or crap fed. All they cared about was having food to eat. At first, AlgiPro was simply distributed in powdered form. Four tablespoons in a glass of water was considered a meal. It was disgusting, but it kept people alive. The food substitutes came later.

When the famine was over, everyone went back to eating real food. AlgiPro plants were shutting down as fast as they had cropped up. So Grier engineered his next great success. He cited the cost of obesity-related health issues among the poor and pitched his plan to solve the problem while helping to fulfill the government's desire that BL create its own economy through work. The BL pack was born. Ironically, Grier was unable to control his own diet and died of a heart attack at age fifty, tipping the scales at three hundred pounds. When Grier died, his son and daughter each inherited enough to put them in the top ten of Forbes' list of wealthiest Americans, right up there with the Kellers and the Waltons.

Jolene pulled into the McDonald's parking lot and shut off the car. Bob and Vera followed her in.

"You don't need to use your vouchers," Jolene said. "I've got this."

"Are you sure?" Vera asked.

"Absolutely. Order what you want."

Bob got his usual Big Mac meal with large fries and a Coke. Vera ordered chicken nuggets, a side salad, and sweet tea. Jolene pressed her thumb to the scanner.

"Aren't you going to get anything?" Vera asked.

"We had a late breakfast," Jolene said. "I'll get an ice cream cone with you all after."

At the condiment table, Vera slipped a handful of ketchup packets into each pocket of her dress. She had asked her friend to put pockets in just for this purpose. She knew Bob was doing the same. Jolene brought their trays over.

A few booths away from them, there was a family with two little boys, each with his own Happy Meal. The kids were refusing to eat their apple slices and demanding more fries. Spoiled, Vera thought. Ungrateful. That's what those kids were.

"Cheers, Mom!" Jolene raised her water and bumped cups with her parents. "Happy Birthday!"

Vera smiled. "Thank you, Jolene," she said. "It means so much to us to spend today with you." Vera opened the BBQ sauce and dunked a nugget in. She put the Ranch and Sweet &

Sour sauces into her pocket. She saw Jolene watching her and trying to decide whether to say anything.

"How is the daycare going?" Vera asked.

"Just fine," Jolene said. "I've got six kids now and I do some evenings here and there."

"Sounds like you could use some help."

"I think I've got it under control," Jolene said. "They are pretty easy. Chris just put a play set in the backyard so we spend a lot of time outside."

"Was it expensive?" Vera asked.

"We got it used," Jolene said. "Have you heard from B.J.?" That was her pet name for Bob, Jr.

"Not yet," Vera said. "I told him we would be at your house, so he'll probably call your phone tonight at about six. That's when he's allowed to make a call."

"I could use more ketchup," Bob said.

"I'll get it for you." Jolene went back to the condiment table.

"What was that?" Bob asked.

"What?"

"Sounds like you could use some help," Bob quoted.

"I didn't mean anything by it," Vera said.

"Don't push her, Vera. Don't do it."

"I'm seventy now. I can go on Medicare and you're already on it. If I get my job back at Kroger, we can move in with Jolene and help out with daycare and the baby."

"What baby?"

"She can have a baby with our help!" Vera said. "You could get a job too. It wouldn't have to pay too much because we wouldn't have to pay rent. We'd make enough money to help with groceries and utilities."

Bob shook his head sharply. Jolene was coming back.

"Everything OK?" Jolene asked. She set down a large handful of ketchup packets.

"Just old married folk jawing over nothing," Bob said.

The steaks were medium rare and thick. Chris had grilled them on his charcoal grill, which Jolene said they got at the Salvation Army. Bob and Vera savored every bite, Bob getting second and third helpings of mashed potatoes and gravy. Jolene brought the cake out with just seven candles on it, one for each decade. They sang "Happy Birthday" and Vera just couldn't stop smiling. She made her wish and blew out the candles. Chris got a tub of vanilla ice cream from the freezer and gave each of them a generous scoop.

When the bowls were scraped clean, Jolene and Chris smiled at each other. She reached out and rested her hand on his. "Chris and I wanted you to be the first to know," she announced proudly. "We are going to have a baby!"

Vera and Bob nearly fell over themselves getting up to hug and congratulate the couple. "I'm so happy for you!" Vera said. "This is the best birthday present in the world."

They asked all the usual questions. The baby was a little girl, due in late summer, and Jolene's morning sickness wasn't too bad. Vera insisted on helping her clear the table.

"You don't have to, Mom. It's your birthday!" Jolene said.

"I want to," Vera said. "We can have some girl time." She ignored Bob's warning glance as Chris led him to the den to watch sports.

Vera loaded the dishwasher while Jolene portioned leftovers on two paper plates and wrapped them with foil. "I'm sending these back with you and Dad," Jolene said. "You can have them for dinner tomorrow."

"Thank you, Jolene. That is so nice of you." Vera helped

Jolene wipe down the countertops.

"Can I ask you something, Mom?"

Vera felt her heart swell. She knew it. Her wish was going to come true. "Sure."

"Would you be willing to stay with me and Chris for a month or two after the baby comes?"

"I would love to," Vera said. It wasn't quite her wish, but after a few months, Jolene would see how useful she was.

"I've already looked into it," Jolene said. "I'll have to submit a form for your temporary leave from BL."

"Sure," Vera said. "Bob could come help too, if you wanted."

"We don't really have the room," Jolene said. "Besides, Dad doesn't change diapers, I've heard you say that more than once."

"I bet he would for a grandchild!" Vera said.

"We only have a twin bed in the second bedroom, so he wouldn't have a place to sleep."

"He could sleep on the couch," Vera said. "He wouldn't mind."

Jolene folded a damp kitchen towel and put it back on the rack. She avoided her mother's eyes. "Mom, you know we don't have the money to feed two extra people for that long," Jolene said. "Chris and I talked about it. He agreed that you could come help for a few months while I figure out how to handle the baby and daycare. We can't afford to let it close for even a week."

Vera knew it then. She knew they would never have a home with Chris and Jolene, but she couldn't stop herself. "I could get a job," she offered, spilling her words out quickly. "I've got plenty of experience. Bob could get one too. He wouldn't need to make much if we were all together. Just find some minimum wage work somewhere. We could help you guys get a bigger place. One with an extra room for us. A big yard for the daycare. I could help you during the day so you could take more kids. Then I could work an evening shift at Kroger. What do you think?"

Jolene's face was impassive. "What happens when you get too old to work?" she asked softly. "How do we keep paying for a bigger place, then? I love you and Dad dearly, but we can't afford to take care of you."

"Then let us stay with you until we can't work," Vera pleaded. "Take us to Peace Out when the time comes. We won't argue."

Jolene didn't answer. She just took the towel off the rack and refolded it.

"It's Chris, isn't it?" Vera demanded. "He's never liked us."

"Don't blame Chris." Jolene's eyes flashed. "We talked about this together. It would never work."

"Then I'll blame you," Vera said coldly. "It's not as though we raised you, fed you, kept a roof over your head until you were eighteen. Not like we didn't dip into our own savings to pay for you to go to college and get that children's degree."

"Early childhood education," Jolene corrected.

"You owe us."

"Owe you?" Jolene gave a bitter laugh. "Do you really want to go there? On second thought, Mom, don't come help with the baby. I wouldn't want to *owe* you anymore than I already do. Get Dad. I'm taking you both home."

"Wait," Vera said, deflating. "Jolene, wait."

Jolene stopped at the edge of the kitchen, her back to Vera.

"Don't pay me no mind, you hear? I just got overexcited.

My birthday and the baby. I know you and Chris do all you can." Vera took two steps forward and put her hands on Jolene's shoulders. "You are building your own family now and that is the important thing. This is your time, not ours."

MARI AND VICTOR

The question before the Court is whether the birth control method known as Gel can be required for all Basic Living recipients. The petitioner has characterized Gel as "reversible sterilization," arguing that it is thusly unconstitutional to impose it upon all BL recipients. The respondent argues that Gel is merely the most effective and inexpensive form of birth control available and is therefore a permissible requisite to place on those receiving the benefits of Basic Living.

This Court has addressed compulsory sterilization in the past. In Skinner v. Oklahoma, Justice Douglas wrote that "[t]he power to sterilize, if exercised, may have subtle, far-reaching and devastating effects. In evil or reckless hands it can cause races or types which are inimical to the dominant group to wither and disappear." 316 U.S. 535 (1942). The Court's primary concern, however, was for the lack of "redemption for the individual whom the law touches." Id.

Before the advent of Gel, sterilization was a surgical, irreversible procedure. Gel is fundamentally different than what was contemplated by Justice Douglas. It is a harmless polymer, which, when injected into the vas deferens of a man or the uterus of a woman, creates a sponge-like lining that prevents the passage of both sperm and eggs, preventing fertilization.

A single injection of solvent dissolves the Gel within a month, restoring fertility. Thus, there is redemption for those whom the law touches. Once they are able to provide for themselves, their reproductive rights will be restored.

While reproductive freedom has continually been upheld as fundamental to the right of privacy, this Court has previously held that a loss of certain rights is an appropriate quid pro quo for the benefits of Basic Living. For example, this Court recently upheld the law requiring Peace Out Directives for all Basic Living recipients. Nelson v. United States 2223 U.S. 42 (2036).

In the case at hand, it is clear that those on Basic Living sap the strength of the government and thusly should not be permitted to create more dependents. Therefore, this Court affirms the decision of the Fifth Circuit and upholds the Gel proviso of the Basic Living Act.

Harper v. United States, 2436 U.S. 115 (2038).

"Marcus!" Mari called.

A little boy with big brown eyes came running over. "Mari!" he said excitedly. "We made an ornament for Christmas!"

The woman working KidCare handed Mari a pipe cleaner bent into a shape that was vaguely star-like. She opened the dutch door so Marcus could get out.

"That's really cool, kid," Mari said. "We can show Mom when she gets home."

Mari was looking forward to Christmas. There was this family in Los Feliz who had sponsored them for three years in a row. The family always included a Christmas card with pictures of them in exotic locations, like in front of a pyramid in Egypt or riding elephants in Thailand. She could count on new clothes for each of them plus one big gift. Last year they had given Marcus a tricycle. She had gotten a charm bracelet, which she never took off. Victor managed to get her a heart charm to add to it on Valentine's Day. She never asked how he got it. She didn't want to know.

The Boys and Girls Club provided blank cards to write thank you notes and mailed them out since donors didn't want BL people to have their addresses. Mari made sure to write a really nice message and had Marcus draw on them. Most people didn't bother, but Mari could tell that her notes made a difference. She didn't know anybody else who got sponsored by the same people every year. She also didn't know anybody else who got such good gifts.

Mari had gone to the Don and used up all her points on a plastic dump truck for Marcus and a Dodgers baseball cap for Victor. She once asked her mom why they had to use their points when people had donated all the stuff anyway. Her mom said the BL Donation Store was supposed to teach them that nothing in life was free.

Mari decided to give her mom the bar of chocolate from Mr. Pao. He had presented it to Mari after she finished her personal statement. Mari wrote about how she had helped care for her brother Marcus since he was a baby and how she hoped to receive training as a nanny. Her test scores were average. Not good enough for a college sponsor. Mr. Pao had been pretty blunt about that.

"Wanna play at the park before we go home?" she asked Marcus.

"Woohoo!" Marcus did his happy dance, a sort of hop wiggle with his arms flapping like a bird. Mari tousled his hair.

Once they got back to their cramped two bedroom apartment, Marcus asked if he could have his special drink. Mari boiled some water and put two slivers of dried orange peel in to soak. "You have to wait until it cools off, OK?"

"OK," he said. After five minutes, Mari used a spoon to put the peels into a second mug of hot water for herself.

The rest of the class was filling out a budgeting worksheet, meant to help them prepare for life off Basic Living. It gave them a hypothetical salary and a list of all the expenses they would have as full citizens. They could choose the apartment with higher rent, but that meant less money for food or transportation. They could choose to board with their employer and have wages docked. Mari thought the assignment just made Basic Living look easier. She was sitting in a chair next to Mr. Pao's desk. It was her turn for a final one-on-one discussion before her Index became available to potential sponsors.

"Have you ever done drugs?" Mr. Pao asked.

"No," Mari said.

"Be honest," Mr. Pao said. "I'm not going to report you if you have. I just need to know."

"I don't do drugs."

"Do you drink alcohol?"

"Where am I gonna get booze?"

"There are ways," Mr. Pao said dryly. "I'll take that as a no."

"What do you care?" Mari asked, curious.

"You'll be tested if you get picked up by a nanny service," Pao said, resting one elbow on his desk. "But I actually have something else in mind for you. Have you ever thought about joining a surrogate farm?"

"Having someone else's babies? Why would I do that?"

"Surrogates make really good money," Mr. Pao said. "You live on the farm, room and board fully covered. You can afford to take classes online or apprentice with the midwives and doulas. After three or four pregnancies, you'll have enough education to get a job and a good amount in the bank to help you if something goes wrong."

"You said I could get in with a nanny service."

"You will," Mr. Pao said. "If you get in with the right family and get the right recommendations, you could work as a nanny for the rest of your life. I think you can do better."

"My scores aren't good enough," Mari said.

"Your scores are average, Mari," Mr. Pao said. "There are plenty of people in college with average scores. They just have parents footing the bill. If you surrogate, you'll have the time and money to go to college."

"Why the change, Pao?" Mari asked suspiciously. "You've been pushing the nanny thing from the beginning."

"I pushed nannying because you look white," Pao said. "There are lots of families who feel more comfortable with a white nanny who speaks English fluently. You fit the bill. The same thing goes for surrogate farms. I met this woman who works for one and she told me about it. There are lots of white people who only want white girls to carry their babies. You'd be in high demand."

"Fuck," Mari said.

"I'll give you that one," Pao said. "It's not like it's conscious or they specifically ask for a white girl. But when people get the portfolio with pictures of surrogates or tour the farm, they invariably choose someone of the same race. Asians pick Asians. Blacks pick blacks. It isn't limited to white people. There are just way more white people in the market for a surrogate."

"Why the fuck would I help those racist motherfuckers have babies?" Mari demanded.

"That's enough Mari. You'll help them because this is the system and this is how you work it. As a nanny, your whole life will be under the thumb of a series of rich women who will make or break your move to a new family when they're done with you. If you're lucky, you'll get one who feels guilty about her wealth. She'll give you a good Christmas bonus and paid vacation. You'll be her personal Don."

"How do you know?"

"My sister is a nanny in Hawaii," Pao said. "One time she got a bag of clothes and half still had tags on them."

"That doesn't sound bad."

"It isn't. She's one of the lucky ones, at least for the next few years. Who knows where she'll end up next? As a surrogate, they borrow your body a few times. You follow the diet and lifestyle restrictions on the farm, but the rest of your time is your own. If you use it to get an education, you'll have a better salary when you're done. You could start a family without worrying about dropping onto BL."

"What about Victor?"

"What about him?"

"Can he get a job at a farm too?"

"He doesn't have the anatomy."

"Come on, Pao-man. You know what I mean."

"He's got too many discipline marks on his record," Pao said. "His best hope is employment within BL. Maybe with a few years of hard work, he could try for a job at a farm."

"Could I visit him?"

"It depends on the policy," Pao said. "I know for some, you don't leave the grounds without supervision. For others you don't leave the grounds at all, especially after you're pregnant. He could visit you, but it would be with a chaperone."

"Why?"

"They'll inject the solvent so you'll be fertile again. The wrong seeds can't be planted, if you get my drift."

Mari flushed. "But he's on Gel," she protested.

"They don't care. It's like a nunnery. Their clients prefer it that way. It's why they pay you so much."

"How much?"

"You'll make between sixty and eighty grand per baby."

"How much do I make as a nanny?"

"Maybe thirty-five a year starting out. Up to fifty thousand after you get some experience and good recommendations. Surrogacy may pay, but you can only do it for five to seven years, so you have to prepare for what you are going to do after."

"Can I think about it?"

"Indexes go live on the first of the year. If you want to do surrogacy, you need to check that option and put something in your essay."

"OK."

"One more thing, Mari. If you truly want a life off BL, you've got to ask yourself if staying with Victor is going to help you achieve that."

"Hell no," Victor said. He had a six-pack of beer next to him on the couch. He offered one to Mari. She refused. Pao had her worried about the drug tests.

"It could be so good for us," Mari said. "Think about the money I could make. I could go to college."

"I'll take care of you."

"How?" Mari demanded. "How can you take care of me?"

"Pao says maybe I can get in with a security company. I stayed outta trouble the last few months. I put it in my essay, like how Pao straightened me out. I do security. You be a nanny. We could make it work."

"What if you don't get it? Then what?"

"Then I try again. I'll get off eventually." Victor pulled Mari onto his lap. He put a beer in her hand.

"I can't, Victor," she said. "They'll give me drug tests."

"Not for months. Alcohol is out of your system in a day. I worked hard for this beer, baby. Drink it."

"What did you do?" she asked, leaning forward to pop the cap off the side of the coffee table.

"You don't need to know," he said.

Mari drank two beers and stayed the night. Victor's mom was on night shift that week and her mom didn't care.

In the morning, Mari checked the box indicating her interest in surrogacy.

"It's conditional," Victor said.

"What does that mean?" Mari asked.

"It means that I got to do good work in a BL job for a year and they'll take me in security."

"For sure?"

"I don't know," Victor said. "I think so. I still have to interview. How about you?"

"I got interviews with two nanny services." Mari stopped in front of KidCare. "And four surrogate farms."

"Damn it, Mari." Victor grabbed her arm. "I told you not to do that."

"I still have to go through medical exams," she said quickly. "I just want to see if I can get in."

"You turn the farms down now."

Mari shook her head. "I won't, Victor."

"The farms are like a prison. They own you. Once you have a baby in you, it's over." He punctuated his words a short jerk of her arm.

"We're in prison now, Victor," Mari pleaded. "BL clothes. BL packs. BL wards."

"I don't see no bars or walls here."

"They don't need them," Mari said. She tried to pull her arm away. "You're hurting me. You said you would never hurt me."

Victor released her. "I'm sorry, *juera*. I didn't mean to grab you. You just made me so mad."

"You touch me like that again and I'm out," Mari said. "I'm not spending my life on BL." Mari rubbed her bicep. His fingers had left marks.

"Me either, babe," Victor said. "Give me a year, I'll get that security job, I promise."

Mari didn't like promises. Her mother's boyfriend had made promises too. "Pao says I can do better than be a nanny."

"You listen to him instead of me?" Victor demanded.

"I listen to me," Mari said. "I gotta do what's best for me."

"It's Pao," Victor said. "He's got into your head."

"He just showed me the possibilities," Mari said. "If you love me, if you want what's best for me, you'll let me do this."

"I can't be without you for that long."

"I have to get Marcus," Mari said, edging toward the KidCare door.

"We have to talk about this, Mari," Victor insisted.

"I'm doing the farm." Mari said, walking away. "Deal with it."

JEREMY AND RACHEL

The police were called to the Angeles National Forest on Friday when hikers discovered a body. While searching the area, police found a homeless encampment with twenty-seven more bodies. The police also found forty empty bottles of vodka. Tested remnants revealed lethal amounts of methanol. Police believe the vodka was delivered in a box found at the scene. The words "You're Welcome!" were scrawled across one cardboard flap. Those words took on a new and sinister meaning as police explored the grisly encampment.

The murders are indicative of a disturbing trend. A National Coalition for the Homeless report states that last year, there were 172 attacks and 32 murders against the homeless. When taken as a percentage of the homeless population, this is the worst series of attacks since the NCH began tracking the crimes over fifty years ago.

While most of the attacks were wilding sprees, perpetrated by middle-class teens with no criminal records, there have been multiple deliberate murders by self-described Peacemakers, who believe that homeless persons' refusal to participate in Basic Living is an unacceptable disturbance of the peace.

The Angeles mass murder has prompted a new call for the

elimination of homelessness in the United States.

"The homeless population dropped by approximately 70% within five years of the establishment of Basic Living wards in every major population center," said Michaela Bart, the executive director for the Washington-based National Coalition for the Homeless. "Those who persist in homelessness are, for the most part, mentally ill or addicts. The time has come to bring them under the protection of BL, which has the resources to provide housing and a variety of treatment services."

An online petition for a California ballot proposition to outlaw homelessness has already received over sixty thousand signatures. The proposition would allow police to detain homeless individuals and transfer them to Basic Living intake facilities.

Mass Murder at Angeles National Forest, Los Angeles Times, 6/12/2042.

Jeremy tried not to be nervous. He smoothed his pants and looked around the waiting room. There were two other people there. An older man with thinning hair. A bony woman with a severe underbite. This was it, he thought. If he couldn't get the money here, Rachel would die.

He had tried everything. No research hospitals were studying Rachel's type of cancer, so no free treatments were available. The clinical trials wanted people who had exhausted other avenues. The hospitals with charitable foundations wouldn't give more than half assistance to a BL denial, which meant Jeremy had to raise fifteen thousand just for Rachel's chemotherapy.

Shana helped him set up a fundraising page on Gift of Life with several photos of Rachel, including a baby picture and one from when she was seven and had lost her two front teeth. Shana said it would help people see Rachel as a real person. Jeremy shared it with all of his friends and they promised to share it with their friends. Over his mother's objections, he had gotten up during a prayer meeting in church and announced his sister's illness and how much money they needed. He ignored the dirty looks he got from the deacons. Two weeks later, the page had collected two thousand dollars, mostly given in ten and twenty dollar increments.

It wasn't enough. It would never be enough. So here he was at Waverley Funding Solutions. Tyler and Shana had tried to talk him out of it. They cornered him at one of the staff parties.

"You're giving away your future," Shana said.

"They'll own you," Tyler said.

"What if it was you guys?" Jeremy responded. "What if Shana was sick? Even if there was just a small chance, wouldn't you do whatever you could to make sure she got that chance?"

"I wouldn't let him do it," Shana said. "I'd Peace Out before he could do it."

"Easy for you to say."

"What does your mom think?" Shana asked.

"I haven't told her." Jeremy finished his beer. "She doesn't need to know." He raised the empty bottle and shook it a little, then ducked around them. He grabbed one more beer, but didn't go back to his friends. He went to his room and made an appointment with Waverley.

A loan officer came for the older man. The bony woman was engrossed in a game on her phone. Jeremy could tell by the way she was hissing and tapping at the screen. He decided to check Rachel's fundraising page. Two thousand dollars. Not a single donation in the last three days. It wasn't right. Rachel was just a kid. Jeremy couldn't understand why BL was denying her treatment. At first, he wanted to call the local news stations and tell the world about this injustice, but Tyler just took him to the Gift of Life website and showed him a dozen pages of BL kids trying to raise money for surgery or chemo or transplants. Some of them didn't even have a single donation.

"Jeremy Fuller?" This loan officer was a woman. She looked just a few years older than Jeremy. Her dark brown hair was severely parted and pulled back into a low bun. He stood up. "I'm Tamsin," she said, holding out her hand. He shook it. "Come with me, please." She led him down a narrow, undecorated hallway to a small office. The window overlooked the parking lot. There was a small aloe plant on the desk and a large ceramic buddha with a fat belly and glass eyes next to it. "Have a seat, Mr. Fuller," she said. "How much do you need?"

Jeremy sat down. "A lot. My sister has cancer," he began.

"Stop right there," Tamsin interrupted. "This is your first time here, so let me explain something. When you made your appointment this morning, I reviewed your Index and, per your authorization, ran it through our assessment program. I do not need to know what the money is for, only how much you need. Once I know that, we can discuss terms."

"I need thirteen thousand dollars."

Tamsin entered the number and ran the program. Jeremy realized he had been drumming his fingers ever since he sat down. He folded his hands in his lap.

"You are approved, Mr. Fuller," Tamsin said.

"I am?" he asked. "Really?"

Tamsin nodded. Jeremy knew he was grinning like an idiot, but he couldn't help it. It would be enough for treatment. He couldn't wait to tell Rachel. "Can you send the money to..." Jeremy stopped talking as Tamsin held up one hand.

"The money will be put in your Index," she said. "What you do with it is up to you. Before I finalize the transaction, however, we have to discuss the terms."

Tamsin went through the options with him. There were laws about the maximum percentage of income that could be garnished by loan companies. He could choose a shorter term, higher percentage loan or one with a longer term and lower percentage. The interest rate was the same, whatever choice he made. In the first five years, he could pay in full at any time and close the account. After that, Waverley would own a percentage of his income for the full term of the loan. That meant if he won the lottery during the term, Waverley got their percentage. If he got a raise, Waverley still got their percentage. If his current income dropped, then the loan term automatically extended until payment in full. He could not participate in Basic Living for the term of the loan. If he became unemployed, he would have four months over the life of the loan to find work. If he did not, Waverley could remove him to one of its work camps until the loan was paid or he obtained employment. If he died, the loan died with him, but he would not be allowed to Peace Out to avoid repayment.

"I am going to record the next portion of our meeting, as required by law." The buddha's eyes turned red. Tamsin continued. "Under the Acosta Usury Act, you must affirm that you lack any tangible asset, such as a house or car, to use as collateral on a traditional loan. Do you affirm?"

"Yes."

"You thereby agree that your physical person shall be used as collateral. Do you affirm?"

"Yes."

"In the event of default, you will be remanded to the custody of Waverley Funding Solutions until such time as your debt is repaid. Do you affirm?"

"Yes," Jeremy said. Everyone knew about companies like

Waverley. Everyone had a friend of a friend who had a relative who spent a year or two in a work camp. But where else could someone like him go for that much money? "I choose the twenty year option."

She held out a touchpad.

Jeremy pressed his thumb against it.

"We're done," Tamsin said briskly. "The funds are deposited. You will notice a drop in your next paycheck. Thanks for doing business with Waverley Funding Solutions. Can you follow the signs back to the lobby?"

"Yes, thank you," Jeremy said. "My sister…"

"Please stop," Tamsin said, her smile growing fixed. "I really don't need to know."

The cut to his pay was way more than he expected. Jeremy had been thinking it would be a percentage of his paycheck, but it wasn't. It was a percentage of his whole pay, before taxes, healthcare, and what he owed to the Enclave for room and board. It pretty much cut his take home income in half. After his phone bill, there wasn't much left. He stopped going to the staff room gatherings, claiming he wasn't in the mood to party. Everyone chipped in for the night's booze, and he simply had nothing to spare.

Jeremy went to his manager and asked for extra shifts, anything to make a little more.

"The Enclave isn't approving overtime these days," the manager said apologetically.

Jeremy couldn't hide his disappointment. "I could really use the money," he said.

"Look, I'm sorry about your situation," the manager said. "I heard what you did for your sister. It was a fine thing, Jeremy. Not many young men would do what you did."

"How could I do anything else? She's my sister."

"Still." The manager wrote out an address on a piece of paper. "Go here. My wife works at the clinic. She'll get you to the top of the plasma donor wait-list. It's good money and you should be able to start in a week or two. Waverley will take their cut, but it should help you get by. I'll schedule your shifts so you have time during the day to go."

Jeremy was already on the wait-list at three clinics. It normally took a year to get off. "I don't know how to thank you," he said, taking the note gratefully.

He started donating plasma a week later. It made him thirsty, but he hadn't noticed any other side effects. The first time he had gotten a huge, painless bruise on his arm. At his next donation, the girl next to him noticed the bruising.

"That looks awful," she said, lowering her tablet. "You should drink more water before. It will help."

"Oh," Jeremy said, looking down at the needle in his arm. "Thanks."

"You're new," she said. "I saw you last week."

"Yeah, I just started."

"I started my sophomore year," she said. "I didn't weigh enough before that! Talk about freshman fifteen." She set her tablet down. She was blonde and petite, her dark brown eyes large and friendly. "A bunch of girls in my sorority do it. They say it helps you lose weight. It's nice to have the extra cash, too. My parents are being kind of stingy with spending money." The girl stretched out her legs. "Do you go to Emory?"

"No," Jeremy said.

"Tech?"

"No."

"Where do you go?"

"I work at Marrietta Enclave," Jeremy said shortly. "I park cars." This was the kind of girl who came to visit her grandparents at the Enclave, currying favor before the big inheritance. This was the kind of girl who knew Daddy would take care of everything until she found the lucky man who would take his place. This was the kind of girl who, if she were inclined, would date guys like Jeremy to strike fear into her mother's heart.

"Oh," the girl said. "You didn't look like..."

"Like what?"

"Nothing," she said. "I just assumed you were in school. Sorry," she said, picking up her tablet.

"You should quit donating," Jeremy said.

"Excuse me?" She looked confused.

"You don't need the money," he said. "There are people who do this to survive and you're taking up a spot that could go to one of them." Jeremy shook his head incredulously. "What do you do? Buy yourself new shoes every month?"

"Look," the girl replied hotly, "if this was supposed to be some kind of charity case thing, they would have put that on the application. Most of us are college students. The people who supposedly *need* the money fail the drug tests or they just don't show up. We're reliable. I put my name on the list and waited just like you, so you can cut the holier than thou crap." She put on a set of headphones that cost more than Jeremy made in a week and pointedly ignored him.

Jeremy never saw her again, and when he asked the check-in guy about the blonde girl who went to Emory, he said she had changed her donation days.

"Here we go again," Jeremy muttered under his breath as the cherry red convertible pulled to a stop at the valet stand.

Grier was kneeling on the driver seat, vomiting onto the trunk. "Mr. Grier?" he asked. "Are you OK?"

Grier was too busy heaving to respond. Jeremy started to call for help.

"Wait," Grier croaked. "Don't call them." He wiped his mouth with the back of his hand. "Water."

Jeremy got a cold bottle from the valet stand and gave it to him.

Grier rinsed his mouth out and drained the bottle. "Just help me get to my room," he slurred.

"I should really call the nurse," Jeremy said.

"Don't," Grier said. "I'll give you a hundred bucks."

"We aren't supposed to solicit money from residents."

"You aren't soliciting anything," Grier barked. He gagged and spewed up all the water he had downed. "I'm offering you the fucking money. Cash."

"I can't leave the valet stand unattended. I could lose my job."

"Damn it," Grier said. "Do what you're told."

"Sir, I believe it is in your best interest if I call the nurse."

Grier grumbled something under his breath. "How long until this fucking valet stand closes?" he demanded.

"Twenty minutes, sir."

"Then take me to my fucking room in twenty minutes."

"I'm not sure..."

Grier fumbled for his wallet and took out a crisp hundred dollar bill.

Jeremy hesitated.

Grier took out a second one.

It was buying a new dress for Rachel. It was being able to bring a backpack of groceries on his next visit home. Jeremy took the money and put it in his pocket. "Would you like another bottle of water, sir?"

"Yes." Grier got out of the car and stumbled around to the front. He leaned against the hood.

Jeremy gave him the water then got out the garden hose. "Sir, I'm going to rinse off your car before the paint gets damaged."

"Fine, fine." Grier said. He drank the water slowly this time, pausing for a minute or two between sips. He did not throw up again.

Jeremy cleaned the car and hosed down the driveway, then got Grier's thumbprint and closed down the valet stand.

"Let's go," Grier said. He took two unsteady steps toward the door and stopped, bending over to rest his hands on his knees.

"I can still call a nurse," Jeremy said.

"Fuck the nurses!" Grier growled.

"They just want to help." Jeremy put Grier's arm around his shoulders and held him at the waist. They made slow progress toward the door.

"What I do is my business," Grier said. "You're a BL kid, aren't you?"

"Yes, sir. Former."

"Look at you. Working hard. Working your way up in the world. Good for you. I got a few grandkids your age and they're worthless. Just waiting to inherit more money, made off of people like you." Grier giggled. It was a hideous sound.

"Me, sir?" He helped Grier into the elevator.

"The AlgiPro empire," Grier said. "Feeding them their own shit and getting paid for it."

Jeremy didn't know how to respond. "What floor, sir?"

Grier pushed a button. "I never would have come here. An Enclave? But her sisters are here. Dozens of them. Alpha

Phi. She loved her sisters. Bridge Club. Book Club. Charity work. My wife was lovely. She was mine. And now she's gone." Grier started to cry.

Jeremy was very uncomfortable. "I'm sorry about your wife, sir." The elevator stopped at the tenth floor. "What room number?"

"The whole floor is mine." The elevator opened into a formal entryway. The ornately carved table held a vase of fresh peonies. "Bedroom that way." Grier gestured and nearly knocked over the vase. "Shit," he said. "Make sure I don't break anything. They're watching me."

"Sir?"

"The maids tell the nurses. The nurses tell my children. They're trying to take control."

Jeremy helped Grier onto his bed. "Are you OK, sir?" he asked.

"Bathroom. Hangover pills."

The en suite bathroom was larger than Jeremy's shared bedroom in the staff quarters. He found the bottle of pills and brought them to Grier with a glass of water.

"What's your name?" Grier asked.

"Jeremy."

"Here," he said, handing him another hundred dollar bill. "Don't tell anyone about this."

"Thank you. Good night, sir."

When he got back to his room, Jeremy had a voicemail from his mother, telling him that Rachel's tumor had shrunk by two centimeters. Jeremy slept soundly for the first time in a month, three hundred dollars tucked into his pillowcase.

Jeremy had splurged on pretty wrapping paper and a bow for Rachel's new dress, tights, and shoes. He held the box on his lap, the backpack of groceries under the seat in front of him. His phone buzzed with a voice message from Waverley Funding Solutions. His first thought was that they had found out about the three hundred dollars. With some trepidation, Jeremy listened to the message.

"Mr. Fuller, this is Tamsin at Waverley Funding Solutions. Your debt has been paid in full. Thank you for your business. Have a nice day."

Jeremy listened to the message three times. He checked his Index four times. The WFS badge was gone. Jeremy had to be sure, so he called her back.

"Tamsin? This is Jeremy Fuller."

"Do you need another loan already?" she asked.

"No, I was just wondering who paid the other one. This isn't a mistake, is it?"

"No mistake," she said. "It was paid by a Mr. Grier this morning."

"So I owe him the money now?"

"I do not know what arrangement you have with Mr. Grier. I suggest you take it up with him. Excuse me, I have to take another call. Goodbye."

HENRY

In the criminal justice system, the Basic Living wards are a primary source of both victims and criminals. In New York City, the dedicated detectives who investigate these crimes are members of an elite squad, known as the Basic Living Unit. These are their stories.
Opening Narration, Series Premiere, Law & Order: BLU, 9/11/2045.

"The last one is steak tartare with capers on toast points," said Mrs. Chang-Siegrist. She passed the platter around. Henry took one and passed the tray to Scott. It was a reddish lump with little green things that looked like tiny footballs. He smelled it gingerly then put the whole thing in his mouth.

Chewing, he whispered to Scott. "This one's the best."

"Speaking with one's mouth full is bad manners," Mrs. Chang-Siegrist said with a disapproving look.

Henry swallowed. "I'm sorry."

"Fortunately, you won't be eating anything at the gala," she said. "I still have a few years before any of you get to sit at a table." She surveyed the freshman class. "You will memorize the list of appetizers that will be served. You will memorize the appetizer ingredients so you can answer any questions about allergens and dietary restrictions. You will come up with unique responses to variations on the question 'Is it good?' There will be a quiz on Friday."

Mrs. Chang-Siegrist dismissed them.

"What do you have next?" Henry asked.

"Choir practice," Scott said. "You?"

"Math tutor," Henry said glumly.

"Hey, at least it's down to the math tutor, right?" Scott said. "That's progress."

"Yeah," Henry said.

"Besides, you're here for art, not math. Who cares if you can do algebra?"

"Colleges."

"Your portfolio is going to be more important than anything else. How's your piece for the auction?" Scott put his tablet in his backpack.

"I don't know if I'll finish in time."

"What is it?"

"I'm stippling on top of a map of the D.C. ward. I don't like it yet. It feels too expected."

"Paint a giant canapé. Vegan and gluten free."

"Maybe I should paint a BL pack. Get those green undertones right."

Scott laughed. "See you later, man."

"See ya."

Henry struggled through an hour of problem sets. Two months until summer vacation. Ms. Keller had him lined up at a series of art camps in Europe. He was one of ten students going along with a chaperone. Scott was headed to music camp in Michigan, but he told Henry he didn't think he would be there long. His mom was finishing school and Scott expected them to be off BL by July.

Henry was going to miss him. Scott was the first person Henry had been able to truly talk with his whole life. He had told Scott everything. About his mother. About Mike.

Mike was holding up his end of the bargain, at least as far as Henry could tell. His mother was taking some sewing classes for retraining. She wouldn't be doing that if she were still working to support her habit. She also faithfully visited him each month, something that really surprised Henry. He enjoyed their time together. There was a sandwich shop around the corner from the school and he would take her there for lunch. He was sure to budget carefully. She never asked him for anything and he never mentioned that he knew she was getting paid to let him be at the school.

Henry went straight from his math tutor to the studio. It was crowded with everyone working on pieces for the auction. It was a pretty good deal. Half the money went into a personal college fund, the rest went to the school. All the high school students participated in the auction. Scott was part of three vocal ensembles offering private performances. Henry hoped Scott would get to do the shows before he got off BL. That way he would get to keep his share of the money.

Henry surveyed his canvas. He dipped his largest brush into a vat of black paint and started painting over everything. He still had three weeks before the gala.

"It looks delicious. How does it taste?" The woman was wearing a strapless aquamarine cocktail dress with layers of taffeta under the bell-shaped skirt.

"Very refreshing," Henry replied. "It's lightly dressed with a lemongrass vinaigrette."

The woman took a shrimp and turned back to her companions. "So I told Jack there is no way we are living in squalor this summer. I don't care if the remodel isn't finished." The woman started complaining about the rental her husband had found in the Hamptons. Another woman joined in with a similar situation on a vacation home in Hawaii. Something to do with cabinets and countertops. Their friends made sympathetic noises. Henry offered the platter to each of them.

Mrs. Chang-Siegrist had instructed them to circulate the room in a clockwise direction. He approached two couples lamenting the expense of private school, the time-consuming nature of club sports, and the proposed law against preference to legacies in college admissions. Three men discussing recent changes to the tax code and in-sourcing were next. Then two women gossiping about board nominations for the Friends of Keller Schools. They lowered their voices and turned down the shrimp. They were gaunt, tan, and drinking champagne.

He saw Ms. Keller talking earnestly with a small group of people. As they cleared his platter, one of the men said his company had decided to pledge a hundred thousand dollars to the Keller Arts School.

Henry went back to the kitchen. He passed Scott on the way. Scott looked perfectly at ease in his black bow-tie and stiff white shirt. "These people are from another planet," Henry said. "Rich white people being rich and white together."

"Just remember they pay the bills," Scott said. "Smile and nod."

Henry got a fresh platter of shrimp and continued his circuit around the room. Three men and a woman were having an animated discussion.

"You can't paint them all with one brush," the woman

said. "BL does a lot of good. My cousin's neighbors were on BL. They retrained and found new jobs in less than a year."

"I'm not talking about people on short-term BL. I'm talking about people who have turned it into a lifestyle. We should cut that part entirely. Maybe a little hunger would motivate them to work like the rest of us." The man stuffed the shrimp in his mouth, his point made.

"We've basically created an under-society of bliss whores and thugs," the second man said. "Someone should round them up and Peace them Out."

Henry started trembling, but the people didn't notice. Henry was nothing. Henry was furniture.

"It's a matter of intelligence," the third man said. "How many tens of millions are on BL? There just aren't enough unskilled jobs left to employ them. So we make up jobs, busywork that makes us feel better about subsidizing their lives. Natural selection isn't working anymore. Think about it. How many kids on BL are good enough for the Keller Schools?" The man answered himself. "Less than a quarter of a percent. Is that worth it?"

"Why are you even here?" The woman was disgusted.

"Supporting the Keller Schools is good PR for our company and an empty table looks bad. We drew the short straws." The man took a second shrimp from Henry's platter.

Henry got out of there fast. Fortunately, there was only one shrimp left on his plate, so he could go straight back to the kitchen. A woman stopped him. "May I have that last one?" she asked.

Henry automatically held out the platter.

"Thank you," the woman said. "You're a freshman, right?" She looked younger than most of the people Henry had served. Beautiful. She was also one of a handful of black people in attendance, her creamy skin as dark as Henry's.

"Yes, ma'am," Henry said.

"When did you start?"

"This year."

"You'll stop hating them," the woman said. "Eventually."

"Ma'am?"

"You're doing a good job of hiding it, but not good enough to fool me." The woman gestured at the people around them. "Listening to them talk can be rough. Most of these people were born into a world of privilege. Oh yes, they work hard, but they don't know what it's like to start at the bottom. They've never eaten algae coated with palatants and labeled meatloaf. They've never been treated with callous indifference."

Henry didn't know how to respond. Mrs. Chang-Siegrist had been vehement in her admonitions against making conversation, especially any conversation that could reflect negatively on the school.

The woman watched Henry's face. "Chang-Siegrist is still at it, isn't she?" The woman laughed. "I was you about ten years ago. I wanted to punch someone. But you'll get over it. I did. Senior year I even made a speech at this thing, thanking them all for their largesse. I managed to work up a few tears for it, too. But then, that is what I trained for."

"I'll never stop hating them." Henry's voice was quiet and firm.

"You will," the woman said. "You will when you become them. That's their goal, you know." A man carrying two drinks came up to the woman and led her away.

Watching her go, Henry realized he had been talking with Alana Baxter. Rising movie star and alum of the Keller Arts School.

VERA AND BOB

People are living longer and consuming more Medicare and Social Security. The math doesn't work and something must be done. But are we as a society ready to tell Gramps that he doesn't get his blood pressure meds or his bypass surgery unless he can pay for it himself? That Grandma can kiss her osteoporosis pills goodbye? That we need to raise the age for collecting Social Security? Can we convince the Q-Tips and blue-hairs that their continued existence is dooming future generations to massive financial obligations?

Everyone knows these programs aren't sustainable, but politicians keep pushing the snooze button on the alarm clock. Well, one of these days that alarm is going to explode. The money just won't be there. Then what? The wealthy ones won't have a problem. But the poor and the middle class? I envision packs of the elderly robbing pharmacies. Demanding dialysis while beating the technician with the tennis ball end of their walkers.

The first step to a solution is legalizing Peace Out. This provides a viable, cost-effective alternative to the current system. The second step is convincing every American, young and old, that it is their duty to society to take that alternative when the time comes.

MSNBC Interview with Lamont Seldon, Author of *The Young Republic*, published 11/1/2023.

Vera's two months with Jolene and Baby Rosie flew by. She changed diapers and made sure Jolene got naps every afternoon. She read to the daycare kids and supervised them on the playset while Jolene breastfed. She made dinners, washed dishes, swept floors, and folded laundry. Vera never said a word about staying longer than the appointed time. Bob visited for one weekend. Rosie found something very soothing about his deep rumbly voice and enjoyed taking naps on his chest. They took a lot of pictures.

On her last day, Vera made a big stew, something Jolene could freeze and use for a few meals. She was ready to go home. At least, that is what she told herself as she watched Rosie sleep in her carseat on the drive back to the ward. Vera had insisted on sitting in the back with the baby. She really did miss Bob, Vera thought to herself. But she would miss that beautiful child too. There was so much hope in a new life. So much ahead. Vera didn't really believe in a god, but she prayed for that child every day. Jolene and Chris would give her a good start, Vera knew that. But then she thought that Bob, Jr. had gotten a good start and look at where he ended up. Vera stroked Rosie's soft cheek.

"Is Rosie still asleep?" Jolene asked.

"Out cold," Vera said.

Bob met them outside the apartment complex. He

opened Vera's door for her and then ducked into the back to see Rosie. She was awake by then and gave her grandpa a toothless grin. "Can you stay a little while?" Bob asked Jolene.

"I've got to get back," she said. "I'm babysitting tonight."

"Well, that's too bad." Bob said it in a silly voice and Rosie giggled. "I wanted to hang out with the most beautiful girls I know."

"We'll see you soon," Jolene promised. "Before I go, I have a surprise for both of you." Jolene got out of the car and popped the trunk. She took out a cardboard box and gave it to Vera. Vera looked inside. It was filled with condiments. Bottles of ketchup, mustard, relish, mayonnaise, horseradish, Tabasco sauce, and a jar of bread and butter pickles. Vera spied a box of Oreos underneath everything. Bob peered over her shoulder.

"Do you like it?" Jolene asked hesitantly.

"It's great," Vera said. "Thank you."

"Thank *you*," Jolene said. "We couldn't have done it without you."

"Any time. You just ask."

"I will."

They exchanged hugs and Jolene drove away, waving goodbye out the window.

"We need a vacation," Bob said.

"Sure," Vera said. "One of those all-inclusive deals like our honeymoon. You win the lotto while I was gone?"

Vera and Bob had opted for a small wedding and spent all their savings on a trip to Cancun. They drank margaritas by the pool every morning and tried all six of the resort restaurants, washing down four-course meals with three kinds of wine. They snorkeled and toured ruins. At the end of the week, they came home sunburned, happy, and pregnant. The experience of a lifetime. Vacations after that were mostly to see family. Free room and board and only the cost of gas to get there. When the kids were old enough, Bob got a loan from Waverley Funding Solutions to pay for a Disney World package. Vera still remembered the kids' faces when they broke the news. Bob, Jr. was speechless. Jolene started crying. Charlie ran around the room in circles until he fell over. They had stocked the hotel room with instant noodles, milk and cereal, a loaf of bread and a jar of peanut butter. Eating inside the park just wasn't in the budget. Vera tried to remember the last vacation they took. It had been Bob's surprise for their anniversary. A weekend in Gatlinburg with tickets to a dinner theater. He had been laid off two months later.

"No lotto," Bob said. "I just heard from Dale Conkle." The Conkles had moved to a ward in California to be closer to their kids. Vera used to work with his wife at the store.

"What does that have to do with a vacation?" Vera asked. "Did they win the lotto?"

"Nope. But these friends they made in California told them a way to take a free vacation every year." Bob paused. "They go to a Peace Out Center. But they don't Peace Out."

"You're kidding," Vera said.

"It's free."

"It's a place people go to die! It's where Charlie died!"

"You said it was the best food you've ever had. The best place you've ever stayed."

"But there are Facilitation meetings every day."

"We would go to those."

"So we would just lie for a week?" Vera shook her head. "I don't know if I could do that."

"You have to. Once you tell them you don't want to Peace Out, you can't stay anymore."

"That doesn't seem right."

"Is this right?" Bob asked, his sweeping arm encompassing their squalid apartment. "Should we be living like this?"

"We have a roof over our heads and food in our bellies," Vera said softly. "We are lucky to live in a country that makes sure we have those things."

Bob's shoulders sagged. "What did I do wrong? How could this happen?"

"You didn't do anything wrong," Vera said reassuringly. "You did everything you could."

"There's no hope for us, Vera. You deserved better." Bob was sounding like he had back when he couldn't find a job. When most of his job applications didn't even garner a polite rejection. When he was told, over and over again, that he didn't have the right skill set or background for the position. Those had been bad times. If Bob was getting like that again, Vera knew what she had to do.

"I got the best when I married you," she said firmly. "I think the Peace Out idea is great. It will be just like Cancun." Vera couldn't help but picture Charlie feeding an apple to a horse. The kind Facilitator who listened to both of them that week. Charlie deep in conversation with a non-existent person in their room at the Center. Charlie's eyes closing as the drugs did their job. Vera didn't know if she could bear going to the Nashville Center again. Not if it was to lie and steal from the people who helped Charlie. "Let's go south! Maybe to the Center in Miami?"

Bob smiled. "Miami sounds perfect."

The time went by quickly. There was so much to plan. Bob researched rail vouchers and found a good deal. It took every point they had, but they did it. Bob filed applications with the Miami Center. There was a two-month wait for non-urgent applicants. A big problem had been their stuff. The only way to get out of their work requirements was to tell their bosses they were going to Peace Out. That meant their apartment might be given to someone else before they got back and in any case would be cleared out and cleaned. They could have asked a friend to help, but Bob and Vera didn't want to tell anybody else what they were doing. Bob said if a lot of people on BL started using Peace Out this way, the rules would be changed. So they brought Jolene in on their plan. She agreed to take them to the station and hold on to their stuff for the week.

Vera tried to remember all the questions the Facilitator had asked Charlie. She hadn't been allowed in all of his sessions, but did get to sit in on a few private and group. She and Bob rehearsed how to respond. It was easier than Vera thought it would be. That scared her a little. But Bob had been in a much better mood ever since Vera agreed to go. Most evenings they would go over their plans while Vera packed their meager belongings. Bob researched all the free activities and sights in Miami. They would have a half day open on each end of the trip. The Peace Out Center was steps from one of the best beaches in town. They wondered if they would have an ocean view. It wouldn't matter. Just to be able to sit on the sand and get their feet wet in the waves would be enough.

At the station, Vera waved until Jolene was a speck in the distance. Bob had chosen an overnight train so they would have plenty of time in Miami before checking in at the Peace Out Center.

"I don't know if I'll be able to sleep tonight," Vera said, putting her bag on the overhead shelf.

"The seats recline," Bob said, pointing.

"It's not that. I'm just excited!"

"Me too," Bob said. "Jolene gave us a little something for the trip." He took out two icy cans of champagne. "Here's to us!"

MARI AND VICTOR

"Basic Living is its own thriving economy. BL recipients man the factories that produce BL clothing. They work the BL stores. They work the BL daycare. They drive the bus lines through the BL wards. All under non-BL management and supervision, of course."

"What about people who refuse to work? The stereotypical BL queen or king who just wants a handout?"

"First off, most people on BL are hardworking Americans seeking a better life for themselves and their families. Furthermore, an attitude of not caring or wanting to work is often a defense mechanism to ward against the depression that comes from being repeatedly denied employment. BL gives a job to everyone who is able to work. Once they build confidence and experience through employment and retraining, BL Career Services will help them find a job outside of BL."

"You haven't answered my question. What about the people who refuse to work?"

"Working is required to receive BL. If they don't work, they don't get BL. If they don't get BL, they go to jail and have to work anyway, but under harsher conditions."

"So I guess the threat of jail is enough incentive to get them to show up to their BL jobs. But why would they try to do a good job? It's not like they can be fired."

"That isn't true, actually. They can be moved from one position to another, less desirable one. There is a natural hierarchy to the jobs. Through hard work they can be promoted to management and get off BL. We also have a points system to encourage productivity."

"Points for what?"

"The little luxuries that are not included in Basic Living."

"So our tax dollars are going to pay for BL luxuries."

"When you are profoundly poor, it is sometimes those little luxuries that give you a sense of self-worth. Earning points gives them pride in their work. A little reward can go a long way."

"Who cares about their sense of pride? Wait, don't answer that. Let's move on to another topic. What if they can't work? Like they are physically or mentally incapable."

"It would have to be really severe. We have jobs that are happily occupied by paraplegics and people with Down Syndrome."

"Let's go there. Really severe."

"Then their social worker would find them a spot in a charitable Enclave. Barring that, they go to Sanctuary."

"So all they have to do is get declared unfit for work and they sail off to a charitable Enclave or Sanctuary, where they are once more freeloaders."

"I wouldn't put it that way."

"How would you put it? Fact: People in Sanctuary don't work and they still get BL."

Interview with Senator Miriam Baxter, architect of the Basic Living Act, The Becker Templin Show, Fox News, 2/22/2045.

Mari accepted the offer from the Palm Springs surrogate farm. It was the closest one to Los Angeles and had a cheap commuter rail so Victor and her family could visit. She liked that it was far enough out of the city to see stars at night. She liked that it had a pool, even though she had never learned how to swim. The recruiter had given her a tour and then sent her off to lunch with three surrogates. The food was unlike anything Mari had ever eaten. A filet of grilled salmon on a bed of wilted spinach with mango chutney. The other girls assured her that they ate like this all the time when they were pregnant. When they weren't, the food was less fancy, but still way better than BL packs. All three girls were former BL. One was almost finished with her dental hygienist certification. One was studying nursing and the third was training with one of the farm's doulas.

The girls worked for room and board and got paid when they did surrogacies. The work was easy. Light housekeeping, gardening, or cooking. They had plenty of time for online courses and could train on-site with nurses, doulas, massage therapists. Pretty much anyone who worked there. Visitors were welcome Thursday through Saturday between the hours of ten and four. The visiting room had a large balcony overlooking the pool with plenty of patio furniture. The room itself had comfortable couches, televisions, board games, and a snack cupboard. There was always a chaperone present. The visiting room was also the girls' hang out spot. They had free run of the expansive grounds, but could only leave the farm for family emergencies, and then with a chaperone. If they were pregnant, they could not leave the grounds at all.

Pao had warned Mari against asking any questions about whether it was hard to be restricted to the farm or the enforced celibacy. Such questions would surely get her rejected. She couldn't help it though, when she saw a wedding ring on one of the girls. "You're married?" she had blurted.

"Yes," the girl said, displaying her ring, the tiny chip of diamond in a plain gold band. "My boyfriend and I got married before I joined the farm."

"How do you... I mean, do you..." Mari stammered.

The girl knew exactly what she was talking about. "We don't," she said simply. "We love each other and wanted to show our commitment through marriage. He visits almost every day. We make it work. It's been three and half years so far," she had said proudly.

At the end of Mari's day of interviews, medical exams and tours, the recruiter had given her an offer. Mari was so overwhelmed she began to cry. The farm was so beautiful and everyone was so nice. She guessed that tears were a pretty common response, because the recruiter had a box of tissues ready.

Mari wouldn't join the farm until she graduated from high school. Her graduation was a condition of her employment. Mari had the option of starting in the summer or fall, but after a huge fight with Victor, she decided to begin right away. Victor accused her of abandoning her family. She shot back that doing surrogacy was the best way she could help them all and that he was the selfish one. Victor raged and punched a hole in the wall, but he didn't touch her. Mari had rinsed off his bruised and bleeding knuckles, but she hadn't changed her mind. She never considered breaking up with him. They had been together since eighth grade. He had been Mari's first everything.

Mari's first day at the farm was busy. First there was a bunch of paperwork. Mari didn't read it; she just applied her thumbprint to the bottom of each page. Then it was a doctor visit. He rubbed a numbing agent on her stomach and squirted a dollop of cold blue gel above her bellybutton. Mari turned her head away when he inserted the needle. She watched the screen instead. She couldn't really tell what he was doing, but it looked like black liquid filling a small balloon. The speckled white section of the balloon was, he informed her, the spongy Gel lining her uterus. She would be fertile in two to four weeks.

Mari was the only one starting in the summer, so the recruiter from before just sat down with her over lunch to go over the rules. There would be a formal orientation in the fall. Mari had heard most of the rules already, but did her best to pay attention. The recruiter gave her a tablet that was hers to keep as long as she lived at the farm. There was a map of the building and the grounds pulled up on the screen. Mari's room was highlighted, but the recruiter dropped her by personally.

Mari's roommate at the farm was just two years older. Brandy was from a ward in Fontana. Her fiery red hair had a good two inches of dark roots. She was curled up in bed with her tablet. Brandy was slender and her belly stuck out like a basketball shoved under her shirt.

Mari put away her meager belongings. There was a soft white dress in the closet that looked about her size. Brandy told her it was the uniform for meeting potential clients.

"Is this your first?" Mari asked.

"Second," she said. "The price goes up after your first. You know, once you've proven yourself."

"That's cool. How long were you here before you got picked?"

"Two weeks. Crazy fast. Of course, they had to wait until the Gel dissolved." Brandy checked the time. "Shit," she said, rolling herself out of bed and slipping on a pair of flip flops. "I'm late for yoga."

"Yoga?"

"Oh yeah, the clients sign you up for all sorts of stuff, put limits on your diet and all that. My couple is Jewish, so I've got to keep kosher the whole pregnancy. I miss bacon, but whatever." Brandy waddled out the door of their room, tying her hair back into a ponytail as she went.

Victor helped himself to a banana from the wooden bowl on the table and a vitamin drink from the fridge. "This is a nice place you got here, Mari," he said, sitting next to her. She had a glass of ice water with a slice of lemon. The sliding glass doors to the balcony were firmly closed. People went outside as little as possible in the summertime. It was like an oven. Even the pool was over ninety degrees.

"Yeah, it's cool," Mari said.

"Can you show me around?" he asked. "Like maybe to your room?"

"It's not allowed. You know that."

"Come on, Mari."

"See that woman over there?" Mari nodded at a hefty woman in a flowery muumuu. "That's Cassie. It's her job to make sure the visitors stay in here."

"We could get around her."

"And get me kicked out?" Mari shook her head. "Not gonna happen, Victor. We can do it. See that couple over there?" She pointed at the girl from her interview. She and her husband were playing Scrabble. "They've been married for more than three years. If they can do it, so can we."

"I don't know, Mari. I love you, I do. But I have needs. And I know you do too." Victor kissed her. Mari kissed him back, feeling the warmth spread through her body. She molded herself against him and his hand slid lower on her back.

"Get a room," Brandy called, throwing a handful of popcorn at them. She was watching a movie with a few other girls.

Mari pulled away, a little embarrassed.

"I would if I could," Victor said, picking popcorn off his shirt and eating it. "Believe me."

That night, Mari confessed to her roommate that she wasn't sure if she could handle being apart from Victor for so long. "I don't know how they do it," she said. "That married couple. How do they do it?"

"They *do* it," Brandy said. "They do it like every chance they get."

"What are you talking about? How?"

"Cassie. Did you know she's my great-aunt? Anyway, she used to be one of us, so she knows how hard it is. You slip her a little cash and she'll slip your boyfriend into the farm for a few hours. It's not cheap. I did it a few times before I broke up with my fucktard boyfriend. He cheated on me with this loser from high school. She posted a picture of them to my Index. Bitch. When I get out of here, I'm going to thrash her fat ass." Brandy suddenly laughed. "Baby boy just kicked."

"Are you fucking with me?" Mari asked.

"What?" Brandy had both hands pressed to her belly, their conversation forgotten.

"About Cassie. Is that for real?"

"Sure. It's a hundred bucks an hour and she lets you use her room. I'm guessing it's the most action Aunt Cassie ever gets."

"I heard these places were total lockdown. A nunnery."

"That's the way the clients have to see it. They don't want their precious baby getting poked in the head by some random schlong. Not for two hundred thousand bucks."

"Can you talk to her for me?"

"Where are you gonna get a hundred dollars? You aren't even in the portfolio yet."

"Victor will get it."

Three weeks later, in the dead of night, Cassie escorted Mari to her small apartment in the basement of the farm. "Your hour starts now," Cassie said. "The bedroom's that way. He's waiting." She lowered her bulk into an overstuffed Barcalounger and turned the TV up.

JEREMY AND RACHEL

How do you tell the difference between the deserving and undeserving? We all know it is our biblical responsibility to be gracious to the poor. Feed the hungry. If we have two tunics give one to the man who has none. But then Paul said if a man will not work he will not eat. So how do we know who deserves our extra tunic?

We don't live in small communities anymore. Oh, you may have the town drunk with slovenly wife and four kids. The church ladies cluck about them all the time and make sure those kids have warm coats and boots for winter. Yet we also have entire neighborhoods of the poor and we have limited contact with them. We have no way of knowing who is deserving and who isn't and we don't have the resources to help them all even if we did.

The government picks up the slack where the church has failed. This is a sad truth. But it does not absolve us of our responsibilities. We must continue to seek out those who deserve our help and serve them with grace and love.

Pastor Graham Talbott, Trinity Broadcasting Network, 8/20/2034

Rachel insisted on trying on her new outfit right away. Jeremy had tried to match the dress to the pink scarf their mother found at the donation store. Rachel was using it to hide the fact that her glossy brown hair was gone. When she woke one morning with a mass of hair left on her pillow, Rachel had asked their mother to shave her head. After two days of wearing a ratty knit cap, their mother had surprised her with the scarf.

Jeremy couldn't really enjoy his visit, though. He couldn't stop thinking about Grier. Why did he pay off Waverley? What did he want? Jeremy listened dutifully as his mother talked about the latest church news and her hope to be hired as church secretary once she finished her secretarial training. He was enthusiastic when Rachel bounded out of the bathroom, twirling in her polka-dotted dress, her scarf tied into a bow on top of her head. He tried not to be distracted while giving a huge, minute-long farewell hug to his kid sister.

The whole ride home, he just kept going over his encounter with Grier. He knew he hadn't mentioned anything about Rachel. Grier must have looked at his Index. Would he be in trouble if people found out? Soliciting from a resident was grounds for immediate dismissal. Jeremy hadn't asked Grier for anything. He couldn't be fired, could he?

Tyler was in their room when Jeremy got back. "The boss man is looking for you," he said without looking up from his tablet.

"Was he mad?" Jeremy asked, heart thudding in his chest.

"No. Why? What did you do?"

"Nothing. I'll tell you about it later." Jeremy went to the manager's office. His boss was on the phone but beckoned him in. Jeremy sat down and waited. His boss put down the phone and rocked back in his chair. "So," he began. "I had a very interesting meeting with Mr. Grier today."

"About me?" Jeremy tried to keep his voice nonchalant.

"Yes. Mr. Grier wants to hire you as his personal assistant."

Jeremy blinked. "Really?"

"I tried to tell him you weren't trained for it. No offense, but Mr. Grier is chairman of a Fortune 100 company. He doesn't care. He told me he would cover tuition for you to get certified and wants you to start right away. You would move to the tenth floor of the Enclave. He has a suite of rooms for his assistant."

"What happened to the last assistant?" Jeremy asked.

"Mr. Grier fired him after his wife died."

"What if he fires me? Would my job here still be available?"

"I can't guarantee that. But you're a hard worker. We would take you back if there was an open spot." The manager could see Jeremy's hesitation. "Listen to me, Jeremy. This is an opportunity that doesn't come up for people like us. Being Mr. Grier's personal assistant will plug you into a totally different world. You'll make connections that will help you for the rest of your career."

"What if I can't do the job?"

"It's not rocket science," the manager said. "If you work as hard as you do as a valet, you'll be fine. Besides, Grier is offering triple your current salary. Free room and board. Full benefits. You can't turn it down, especially not with your sister's situation."

Jeremy thought for a minute. "You're right," he finally said. "I guess I do have to try."

"Grier sent me all the paperwork." His manager gave him a tablet. "Once you submit it, your thumbprint will give you access to the 10th floor. Grier is away on business, but said you should get settled in right away and learn the calendaring program and phone protocols. It's all in the tablet. He'll be back Monday. Call the maid service after you pack. They'll send someone to help you move and show you where your rooms are."

Tyler was still in their room when Jeremy got back. "What's going on?" he asked as Jeremy started pulling his clothes from the closet and dumping them on the bed. "Are you fired? Are you OK?"

"Grier," Jeremy said dazedly. "Grier hired me to be his personal assistant." He shoved clothes into his backpack.

"Holy shit."

"Yeah. I helped him out a few nights ago when he puked on his car."

"Un-fucking-believable. You're like one of those movies on the Hallmark Channel."

"Whatever, man." Jeremy held up the tablet the manager had given him. "I've got to fill out some forms."

"Don't forget about us, Mr. Big Time."

"You don't know what you're getting yourself into." The maid shook her head, leading him to a door near the master bedroom. Her frizzy hair was streaked with grey and shellacked into a bun. "Mr. Grier isn't all there you know. I think it's Alzheimer's like my father, but the family won't say. It's so sad. They ask me to keep an eye on him, make sure he is doing OK. Sweet people." She opened the door. "These rooms are yours."

The suite was furnished and decorated like the rest of the penthouse. It didn't seem real. Jeremy dropped his backpack onto the couch.

"Mr. Grier's last assistant never used that kitchen," the

maid said.

"Did you know him?"

"Oh yeah," she said. "Nice guy. Really cared for Mr. Grier. When the drinking got bad, he was the one who told the family. That's when Mr. Grier fired him." The maid pulled the curtains open.

"What's he doing now?"

"The family set him up with another job. Like I said, they are sweet people." The maid excused herself.

A few minutes later, a phone started ringing. Jeremy found an old-fashioned rotary phone on an end table.

"Hello?"

"Jer? It's Shana. There's a woman here to see you. Shall I send her up?"

"Who is she?"

Jeremy could hear the woman's voice in the background. "Tell him Mr. Grier hired me to help him transition to the new job."

"I heard that," Jeremy said. "Send her up."

"Will do," Shana said. "Congrats, by the way. Tyler told me everything."

"I'm a consultant with Singh Protocol," the woman said, taking Jeremy's measurements and jotting them down in her notebook. "We work with aspiring politicians, executives who want their mistresses classed up, and whimsical billionaires who hire uneducated valets as personal assistants." The woman took Jeremy's picture. "Fortunately, you are fairly good-looking. That should smooth over minor gaffes as long as you smile." The woman eyed him speculatively. "You need a haircut." She started making phone calls. "You've got some tutorials to do, don't you?"

For the next four days, the woman from Singh Protocol came over before breakfast and left after dinner. They took meals in the room. Jeremy learned table manners and how to order properly. He learned how to manage the calendar and skimmed through something she called a Farley file. It had thousands of names and personal details, like whether the person had kids or a hobby. The Singh woman told him there was no need to memorize anyone outside the first circle. She quizzed him on who should be put straight through to Mr. Grier and how to deflect those who should be ignored. He learned where Grier liked his dry cleaning done, how he took his coffee, when he last had the oil changed in his car. The third afternoon a man arrived from Macy's with a rack of clothes and shoes. On the last night, the Singh woman ordered a bottle of champagne with dinner. She poured two glasses and handed one to Jeremy.

"You're a quick study," she said. "I think you'll make it through the week without getting fired."

"Um, thanks?" They clinked glasses and drank.

"Actually, I'm surprised no college took you on."

"I don't do so well on tests."

"You've done fine on mine."

"That's different." Jeremy said. "I used to throw up before every test. I could barely write my name, let alone answer the questions."

"Don't worry. The tests with this job will all be practical," she said. "People like Mr. Grier are used to getting what they want, when they want it, and they want it done a certain way. If you fail in that, in any little detail, you have to be prepared to face the consequences. You'll be yelled at. You'll be belittled. If your mistakes add up, you'll be fired."

"That doesn't make me feel better."

"My job is to prepare you for your job," she said. "I'm not going to sugarcoat it. You will be at Mr. Grier's beck and call. You will work far beyond regular working hours. You will work weekends and holidays. You will find yourself doing things that seem ridiculous, but are of vast importance to Mr. Grier for unfathomable reasons. You will take whatever verbal abuse he dishes out and never talk back to him. And any time you think you can't take it anymore, any time you want to go back to your winning career as a valet, you'll remember that you have a little sister, dying of cancer, and your paycheck is what's keeping her alive."

HENRY

I am the oldest of three. When we were kids, I made up games for us to play. Board games. Card games. Tag and hide and seek. I loved to win. So any time it looked like the game wasn't going my way, I would change the rules. And if they didn't accept it? If they claimed I was cheating? Well, I was bigger than them. They didn't have much choice. But that was the hard way.

Over time, I figured out that the more subtle the rule I "remembered," the more gently the new rule changed things in my favor, the more likely my siblings were to accept the change without protest.

Isn't that where we are today? People like me tirelessly work to make sure the rules come out in our favor. Why? Because we can. Because the corporations and interest groups behind us have the money and the power to make it happen. And what of the poor siblings, fighting so hard to win a game that is designed to make them lose? Well, there is this blind faith in capitalism. This blind belief in the American dream. And there are those few who actually make it happen for themselves. Those ones get a lot of publicity.

There are people who know the game is rigged, but John Q. Public thinks those people are Chicken Littles, claiming the sky is falling. It is

impossible to explain how one tiny change in the law will have an impact on anything, because, taken alone, it won't. That's the beauty of it.
Basic Living will pass. I have no doubt of that. Depending on who you talk to, Basic Living either enables or punishes the entitlement set. Maybe it is a bit of both. Who cares? While debates over Basic Living keep the masses focused, the power brokers quietly stack the deck.
notahottentot, r/Basic Living, Reddit, 2/21/2033.

Henry stood at the podium staring at the speech in his hands. Alana Baxter had been right. It had taken a while, but his hatred for the people sitting at the tables in front of him had transformed into something else. Most were just trying to help. They opened their pocketbooks so that kids like him had a chance to attain the education and connections they were born with. How could he hate them for that? Their motivation for giving didn't matter. What mattered was that he was standing in front of them with a full scholarship to Columbia University.

Mrs. Chang-Siegrist had coached him on his speech. He was supposed to talk about how the Keller Arts School impacted his life and how honored he was to receive the Caughey Prize. He had learned that Mrs. Chang-Siegrist was a volunteer. One of the rich housewives who was a member of the Friends of Keller School. They raised millions with their annual gala, parading the older students around like rare specimens.

Everyone was waiting for Henry to begin. Mrs. Keller was at a table near the front. She gave him an encouraging nod. Scott was sitting next to her, digging into a chocolate mousse. Henry had been allowed to have a guest, but he hadn't chosen his mother. She would have been uncomfortable. Taking her out of the ward and into the gala would have been cruel. At least that is what he told himself.

Henry had been home only once in the last four years. During his junior year, his mother fainted at work. He had gotten permission to take the train down to see her. Henry had been amazed at how strange the ward looked. The streets seemed more narrow. Everything was shabby and dirty. Everyone looked vaguely threatening. He felt like an outsider. He had become an outsider.

At the hospital, the doctor said it was just fatigue. A few days rest and his mother would be fine. Henry wasn't sure the doctor was telling the truth. He could see it in the papery texture of his mother's skin and the careful way she moved. He talked with Mrs. Keller about it the next day, told her he was worrying too much to focus on school. She helped Henry's mom get moved to a less strenuous job at the Don.

On his mother's next visit she told him all about the new job, sorting and tagging old clothes, housewares, and toys. A lot of it was trash. Shirts with tears or stains, chipped plates, board games with missing pieces. The younger workers stocked the racks and shelves. She got to sit in a padded office chair at a long table. Her clothes were newer now. As a sorter, she got first pick at the donations and had plenty of points from the Keller School. She proudly showed off the shimmery teal sweater she had found. It was low cut and tight, revealing spidery stretch marks on her stomach. When she sat down, a bulge of flesh spilled over the top of her jeans. Her heels were gold and at least five inches high. She always dressed up for their visits and he wished that she wouldn't.

Henry was right not to invite his mother to the gala, he told himself once more. She would have been out of place. As out of place as he was back at the ward. Besides, Henry saw

Scott way more than he saw his mom, even though Scott had transferred to a public high school when he got off BL.

Scott's mother had been hired as the second personal assistant to the wife of a hedge fund manager. She wasn't around much, so Scott was free to explore New York with Henry. Scott was ranked first in his class and headed to Stanford in the fall. He had tried to convince Henry to apply to the art schools in San Francisco, but Henry wanted to stay close to his mother. She was the only family he had and Henry had convinced himself that their monthly visits were helping keep her habit under control.

Henry set his speech on the podium and began. "Four years ago, I was a boy with no future. At least, no future that any of you would want for your children. Living on BL, child to a single mother. I escaped from my world through art. I used my points on an art history textbook and memorized it. I taught myself to draw." Mrs. Chang-Siegrist had cut the part about scrounging for supplies. She didn't want to highlight the lack of art in BL schools. The focus was fundraising for the *Keller* Arts School.

"Of course, I knew about the Keller Schools. I also knew someone with my grades never stood a chance of gaining entry. But when Mrs. Keller saw my drawings, she offered me a spot at this wonderful place I have called home ever since." Mrs. Chang-Siegrist had also cut the part about Mike's involvement. It distracted from the message.

"The Keller Schools do not simply provide a good education, they provide a structured and caring environment. When a difficult home situation was distracting from my studies, Mrs. Keller found a way to help. When I wasn't able to handle the schoolwork, she brought in special tutors to get my academics up to speed. My teachers and resident advisors have become like family. They are all dedicated to the mission of the Keller Schools: To help kids like me achieve a life off Basic Living.

"This place changes lives and they rely on your help to do so. A huge thank you to the Friends of Keller Schools, and to all of you here today for showing your support. Because of you, I now have a future worth living. My name is Henry, and I am this year's Caughey Prize recipient. I will be studying visual arts at Columbia University." The audience clapped. Scott let out a cheer and a few others followed suit.

Henry spent the rest of the evening being introduced to donors and answering the same questions over and over again. During a lull, Henry ducked into the atrium. The walls were lined with tables of silent auction items, the winners circled in red on the bid sheets. Henry decided to find his submission and see how much it had gone for. The Caughey Prize covered tuition, room, and board, but he still had to pay for books and incidentals. The three canvases had their own table. The highest bid was just over ten thousand dollars, the same buyer as the previous years, a guy named Morris.

"Hiding?" A woman stopped next to him, holding a glass of red wine.

Startled, Henry looked down at her. She was petite, her head barely reaching Henry's shoulders even in high heels. Her dark brown hair was swept up and curled, her eyes a gold-flecked green with an exotic tilt that matched her flawless olive skin. She wore a black calf-length dress and no jewelry. Henry felt a sudden urge to paint her. The diffident Henry was gone, erased by a string of girlfriends and a growing confidence in his prowess as an artist. "Saying goodbye," he said. "It's hard to let my work go." He indicated the paintings.

"They're amazing," she said sincerely. "You are very

talented."

"Thank you," he said. "I'm Henry."

"I know." She smiled. "I'm Irene." She turned her gaze back to the paintings.

Irene must have graduated before he got to the school, Henry thought. He would have remembered her. "Want to get out of here?" he asked. "I'm tired of shaking hands and making small talk."

"Alas, I am here with someone else." Irene's eyes danced and her smile sent a thrill through Henry's spine. "I *am* flattered by the invitation, though. Good luck to you Henry. I'm sure we'll meet again."

He watched her go. Of course a girl like that wasn't at the gala alone. Henry decided to find Scott and drink as much free booze as possible.

"We need some money." Mike was matter of fact. "Two hundred bucks cash should do it."

The first call came during Henry's freshman year of college. Mike asking about the art he sold during high school and wanting his cut. Henry tried to explain that the money was in his college account and could only be used on books and art supplies, but Mike didn't care. He gave Henry a month to make the first payment.

So Henry got a job at Columbia's call center, contacting university alumni and parents to ask for donations. They had a file on each prospect with things like giving history, major, and primary activities. That way Henry could try to finagle a donation for a particular cause if the prospect wouldn't donate to the general fund.

Henry hated the days when they called alums from the early twenties. Too many of them were dead. Columbia's database cross-referenced the National Index, so Henry knew when he was calling a dead person. They always waited about a month after death before calling. Henry had to offer condolences and make notes in the file about the logical next-of-kin to receive future calls. They never asked for money on those calls. Since Henry got bonuses when he hit certain dollar amounts, he viewed the death calls as a waste of time. But he managed to get two hundred dollars together the first month.

On his mother's next visit, Henry had given her an envelope of cash. She put it in her purse without a word. Henry often wondered how much his mother knew about his arrangement with Mike. Did she just accept that her life was better now? Did she want to know why? Did it even make a difference to her?

Of course, Mike's calls had continued even after Henry paid the ten percent off his auction sales. The calls never came too close together, and Mike always called it an advance against Henry's future success.

"Two hundred bucks," Mike repeated. "It's your momma's birthday."

"I don't have it right now," Henry said. Henry had been spending his earnings on canvas and paint. As a junior, he was getting his own room at the student showcase that spring. Henry was practically living in the studio.

"Your momma's coming up next week. You better have it by then."

"I can't do it," Henry said. "There's no way I can make that much before next week."

"Find a way," Mike said, ending the call.

Angry and frustrated, Henry called Scott and told him what was going on.

"No problem," Scott said. "I'll loan you the money. You

pay me back when you can."

"I don't want to borrow money from you," Henry said. "That's not why I called."

"This is what friends are for," Scott said. "Besides, my Mom's new husband is really trying to get on my good side."

"How is that going?"

"He gives me a great allowance. And he bought me a car."

"Damn."

"It's done," Scott said. "I just sent you the money."

"You didn't have to do that."

"Yes, I did," Scott said.

"I'll pay you back as soon as the showcase is over."

"Whenever," Scott said. "Don't worry about it."

"Thanks, man." There was a moment of silence. "So what's up with you?" Henry asked. "It's been a while."

"I got the internship at Peace Out LA!"

"That's awesome!" Henry's enthusiasm was genuine. Scott had been really disappointed when Peace Out put him on the wait list. His only consolation had been that only one Stanford premed had actually gotten in, and it was at the Center in Arkansas. Scott worked hard to believe that a summer internship in Arkansas was worse than no internship at all.

"Someone out there is watching out for me," Scott said. "I thought I was going to have to take the job with my stepdad. I don't know how the spot opened up."

"Don't question it," Henry said.

"I'm not. I can't wait to start."

"Where's Evelyn working this summer?"

"London. But it doesn't matter. We broke up."

"I'm sorry, man. You guys were good together."

"I broke it off with her. I'm OK. She started acting weird after I got the internship. Possessive. Too much crazy to be worth it, you know?" Scott laughed. "Of course you know. I don't even bother learning the names of your girls. They change too quickly."

"It's not like I want it like that," Henry said. "I just don't feel a connection. It's convenient. It's fun. But it isn't real."

"You're still looking for Irene." Scott said.

Henry didn't answer. In the weeks after the gala he had searched for her. Pored through the gala guest list, but there was no Irene listed. Searched the Keller alumni database and the National Index with no luck. He still looked for her every time he got on the subway or walked through Central Park. He had sketched her portrait on a piece of paper and kept it folded in his wallet. She appeared in all of his paintings. The green-gold of her eyes in a grassy field. The curve of her cheek in the fruit of a still life.

"You've got to get over her," Scott said.

"I know."

"She was already with someone. She could be married with a kid by now."

"I know," Henry said.

VERA AND BOB

Amnesty for illegals who register on the Index by the end of the year? WTF? Why not send them home?!
@BeckerT, 3/27/2037.

The intake was surprisingly easy. The bare facts on their Index seemed to satisfy the Facilitator. Vera was a little put out. She was glad she didn't have to lie, but also wanted to defend her existence, that being seventy and on BL wasn't reason enough to die. Then an attendant had shown them to their room and Vera's discontent vanished. She and Bob could scarcely maintain their somber faces. As soon as the door closed behind the attendant, Bob grinned wide enough to show a missing molar and Vera dissolved into shocked laughter. The room was like something out of a movie, the gauzy curtains billowing in the ocean breeze.

"Shh," admonished Bob. "She'll hear us."

"I can't stop," Vera gasped.

Bob scooped her up and carried her toward the bed.

"Your back!" she protested.

Bob lowered her onto the quilted comforter.

"*Bienvenido a* Miami!" he declared. "I saw that on a sign at the train station."

"Lay down," Vera ordered. "You gotta feel this bed."

Bob stretched out next to her. Both of them still had their shoes on. They stared at the ceiling fan, which was twirling lazily above their heads. "How long before dinner?" Bob asked.

"I think we have an hour," Vera said.

"Then let's check out the rest of this room. Maybe shower and change?" They were still in the clothes from the train ride the night before.

"Sounds good to me."

While Bob took a shower, Vera went through every drawer and closet. There were plush white bathrobes and slippers in the closet. The drawers were empty. There was a little station with a coffeemaker, mugs, and two chocolate chip cookies. Vera munched on one while she examined the vanity. There was a tray with Q-tips, cotton balls, sunscreen and aloe vera lotion. She went out to the balcony and leaned on the railing. The Center was a hundred feet from the beach and their view was more than she had hoped for.

There was a rock waterfall right under the balcony and carefully landscaped paths leading to the pool, hot tub and ocean. The beach was dotted with chairs and umbrellas. Vera saw the backs of five people in wheelchairs lined up under the shade of a large cabana, an attendant sitting nearby. She saw a couple holding hands and walking back toward the Center. They looked older than Vera and Bob, but were probably Pledge 70. Must be, she thought.

She and Bob had never taken the pledge. What did it

matter to them? They weren't in a position to get the Pledge 70 discounts and tax breaks. Besides, Vera knew she could never have gone through with it. In her mind, Peacing Out was for people with serious health problems. Terminal cases and people like Charlie. She didn't need the shame and consequences of being a reneger.

"Your turn, Hon." Bob was dressed already and eating the other cookie. He offered her half.

"Already ate mine," she said. "Thanks."

After Vera's shower, they examined the schedule of facilitation sessions. It wasn't onerous, just two sessions a day, a mix of individual, couple, and group. They were scheduled to Peace Out together.

"It's dinnertime," Bob said. "Shall we?" He offered her his arm.

By the third day Vera wished they never had to leave. She enjoyed the luxury of real food for every meal and the silky sheets, but the best part was Facilitation. Everyone was so kind and understanding. She poured her heart out about Jolene and the baby at her last private session, how she maybe wouldn't even be Peacing Out if Jolene had been willing to let them move in. It was part of the story she and Bob concocted, but it was also close to the truth. Vera cried through half the session, the Facilitator offering her a box of tissues. She wondered if the group session that night would be the same.

The session was being conducted around a fire pit on the beach. It was still an hour before sunset, but the weather had cooled enough that Vera was glad she brought a sweater. She and Bob sat on a driftwood bench. They watched as an attendant carried a young man out. His withered legs dangled. The attendant settled the young man in a beach chair and draped a blanket on his lap. Vera thought about greeting him, but the young man kept his gaze fixed on the ocean. The attendant returned at the elbow of an elderly woman, helping her get her walker through the sand. An odd-looking woman trailed after them, clutching a ragged stuffed rabbit. She sat near the elderly woman, grunting and rocking back and forth. She twisted one of the rabbit ears in a rhythmic motion. The last member of the group was a middle-aged man. He looked perfectly healthy. Muscular, even.

The Facilitator was a woman, white strands visible in her long black hair. She started by asking them to introduce themselves.

The young man was first. "I'm Mitch. I have cancer."

"Is there anything more you'd like to share?" the Facilitator encouraged.

"No."

She smiled. "That's fine. Thank you, Mitch. Who's next?"

Bob raised his hand. "I'm Bob and this is my wife Vera. We've lived in Nashville all our lives. We've been on BL ever since I lost my job. We're both 70 now and that's why we're here."

"I'm Greg," the fit-looking man said. "I'm a personal trainer. Used to be anyway. My kidneys don't work anymore. I can't afford to buy a new one and my insurance doesn't cover dialysis. The funding companies turned me down. Said I was too old to be a good investment. Between savings, family, and friends, I bought another year of life. It gave me time to get used to the idea of Peacing Out. So here I am. I'll be dead in a week anyway, but I might as well do it here, right?" His laugh was a short bark that made Vera cringe.

The elderly woman with the walker spoke next. "I'm Maggie and this is my daughter Ella. She's severely autistic.

Doesn't really talk. I had a stroke last week and my doctor doesn't think I'll live out the month. My other kids say they'll take turns with her, but they tried after my first stroke and she was back with me in no time. Ella can be difficult. After I go, they'll put her in Sanctuary. She won't do well in a place like that. It's better this way."

Ella had stopped rocking at the sound of her mother's voice. She seemed to notice the ocean for the first time.

"She's gonna bolt," Maggie warned. Two seconds later, Ella headed for the waves, moving faster than Vera expected. The attendant chased after her and caught her around the waist. Ella thrashed in his arms, butting her head into his face. The attendant threw Ella over one shoulder and brought her back to the circle. He put her in her seat and stepped back, one hand pressed against his nose, blood dripping between his fingers.

"Stay," Maggie ordered.

Ella stared at the flames, rubbing the bunny against her cheek and moaning, but she didn't try to get up again.

"Thank you Maggie," the Facilitator said, as if the interruption had never occurred. "Friends, tonight's session is going to be about Peacing In. I can see that phrase is new to many of you. When you Peace Out, you will Peace In to something else. There are many different beliefs on what comes next, but it is something we like to explore."

"What the fuck?" Mitch exclaimed. "Who the fuck cares what happens after?"

"We do," the Facilitator said. "We find that people who choose to leave this world on their own terms tend to have strong beliefs on the matter. What do you think?"

"I think I'll become a rotting meat bag." Mitch's face was hollow, the dark circles under his eyes visible even in the waning sunlight. His baldness was concealed by a baseball cap.

"What about your soul?"

"It will return to the nothing from whence it came."

"Do you find comfort in this?"

"Jesus, who comes up with these questions?" Mitch scoffed. "I'm done."

"Thank you for sharing, Mitch." The Facilitator turned to Greg. "What about you? What do you believe you'll be Peacing In to?"

Greg thought for a moment. "I believe it will be an ending, not a new beginning. I had no awareness before birth, and I believe I will have no awareness after death. I'm just glad I had time to accept the inevitability of my death. To come to peace with it, no pun intended. I've lived a hell of a life. I've got no regrets."

"Except wishing you had enough money for a kidney," Mitch muttered. Vera heard him over the sound of the waves and the crackling fire, but only because she was sitting right next to him.

"What about you, Vera?" the Facilitator asked.

"I don't know," she replied. "I haven't thought about it really."

"And yet, you are ready to end your time on earth just a few days from now?" There was a hint of uncertainty in the Facilitator's voice.

Bob put his hand on Vera's thigh and gently squeezed. Vera knew she had to correct herself. "What I mean, is that I have no control over what happens after I die. So I'm here to take control over what I can. Isn't that what Peace Out is all about?" Bob gave her another squeeze and removed his hand.

"It is," the Facilitator said. "But surely you have some belief about what comes next."

"Heaven," Vera said. "At least that's what I hope for. Doesn't everyone hope for that?"

"Heaven," Bob echoed, "and a God loving enough to let us in."

MARI AND VICTOR

"The goal of Basic Living is to get people off of Basic Living, is that correct?"

"Yes."

"But in twenty-five years, statistics show that the number of people on Basic Living has been fairly static."

"That is actually a sign of BL's success, especially since we are still recovering from the Recession. On previous welfare systems, the number of dependents went up every year."

"Our statistics also show that 75% of the people who get off BL end up back on it within five years."

"That is also a misleading statistic. What it really means is that fully a quarter of former BL recipients are able to integrate with working society. As for the others, well, unfortunately, there is no changing human nature. Many people on BL make poor life choices, have mental health issues or disabilities, or find they are unable to function in a traditional job setting. For those people, a life on BL is their best and only option. We provide jobs for them within the BL system to fulfill their work requirements. They don't have to manage money as everything is rationed."

"Some accuse BL of being the embodiment of the nanny state."

"We don't deny it. BL is indeed a nanny for individuals who are not yet capable of surviving in today's society on their own. Is that a bad thing? Where would they be otherwise? What would they be doing otherwise? Do we want them turning to lives of crime to survive? Do we want them dying in the streets? This is America, not some third world country."

CNN Interview with Hillary Moore, Secretary of Health and Human Services, 11/1/2060.

This time, Mari thought. This time I'll get picked. She was wearing the white dress provided by the farm and had carefully brushed her hair. On the advice of some of the more experienced surrogates, she wore no makeup, just a dab of lip gloss. The goal was to look wholesome. The kind of person a couple would trust to bear their child. She had met with three potential clients since the doctor declared her uterus clear and been rejected each time.

Mari waited in a comfortably furnished room. Classical music was playing in the background. One wall held a cork board full of birth announcements, most featuring naked babies positioned on fuzzy blankets. Mari decided not to sit down and risk wrinkling her dress. According to the clock on the wall, the clients were late. This was normal.

After a while, there was a soft knock on the door. Mari's client liaison came in, followed by an attractive couple. The woman was wearing a yellow sundress and espadrilles. The man was in khaki shorts, a polo shirt and loafers.

"Mari, this is Mrs. Bell. She saw your profile in the portfolio and asked to meet you."

Mari stood up and shook the woman's hand. "Mrs. Bell, it's nice to meet you." She held her hand out to the man. "You too, Mr. Bell."

"Oh no," Mrs. Bell said. "This is my friend, Drake Cleager."

"So sorry, Mr. Cleager." Mari blushed and hoped she hadn't ruined her chances.

"An easy mistake," he said. "You can call me Drake. You can call her Alyssa."

"Drake has used our farm twice," the liaison said. "How are the kiddos?"

"Great!" he replied. "Patrick took them to the zoo this morning so I could be here."

"Well, you know we are here for you if you decide to have another."

"We're still in talks," Drake said with a dismissive wave of his hand. "Patrick doesn't want to do the diaper phase again. In the meantime, though, I get to help this lovely woman and her husband navigate the intricacies of choosing a surrogate."

"Well, I'm sure you would like to get to know Mari a little more," the liaison said.

Alyssa smiled at Mari. "I would," she said. "Can you tell me about yourself? Something not in your profile?"

That was an easy one. "I like to cook," Mari said. "I've been helping in the kitchen here. Just prep work and clean up mostly, but I'm learning a lot."

"Do you have a boyfriend?"

Mari had been warned that potential clients would fully vet her Index, so she answered honestly. "I do. We have been together since junior high."

"Tell me about him."

'He lives in Los Angeles. We have supervised visitation every weekend."

"Is he on BL?"

"Yes, but he is in training to become a security officer."

"How long have you been at the farm?"

"Four months."

"Have you met with other potential clients?"

"Yes."

"Do you know why you were not selected?"

"Yes. Two chose a proven surrogate and the third chose a less expensive farm in Bakersfield."

"Ugh," Drake said. "Patrick and I visited that place when we started out. The supervision there is terrible. I heard a girl got caught doing bliss. *While* pregnant! Can you imagine? They paid out a huge settlement, of course."

"As for the others, they were parents seeking just one more child," the liaison said. "The girls they used in the past aged out of our program, so it made sense for them to go with a proven surrogate. Drake can tell you, it is a very positive thing to have continuity. Mari is just 18. If you want three children spaced out, you could even reserve her for the next four or five years. It ensures that she is available when you want to grow your family. Otherwise, she might be booked with another client."

"What if she quits or finds another job?" Alyssa asked.

"Then you receive a full refund for your reserve payments."

Alyssa addressed Mari. "Are you comfortable with the lifestyle here?"

"Yes," Mari said. "The farm is a great place to live. I've made some wonderful friends. I do miss my mom and little brother, but they visit me as often as they can."

"What about your boyfriend?"

"It isn't easy. But he knows this is what is best for us." Mari didn't mention that Victor had asked her to leave during their last tryst, tangled in Cassie's faded sheets. He said a job was already waiting for him working security at a shopping center near the ward. She could get a job there too. A lot of the stores were hiring clerks. Mari had demanded to know if he truly believed that was going to be a good future for them. For their children. Victor said it would be good enough and who did she think she was anyway, did she think she was better than him? The fight got loud enough that Cassie came back and banged on the door, telling them to shut the fuck up. Mari had dressed quietly, and told Victor that if he ever asked her to leave again it would be over between them.

Mari rearranged the folds of her dress and waited for Alyssa to ask another question.

"Why did you choose to surrogate?" Alyssa asked.

"The real reason," Drake added, "not a variation on the theme in every profile."

Mari looked to the liaison for guidance. The woman's face gave Mari no indication of how she should answer. She decided to tell the truth.

"I grew up on BL," Mari said. "I don't want to live like that ever again. This farm is my way out. I will do the best job I can to take care of your baby, because I need the money to go to college and get a good job. Because I will *never* go on BL again. Never." Mari could tell from the way the liaison was gripping the arm of the chair that maybe she had been too honest.

"I like her," Alyssa said. "She's the first one that hasn't given me some BS answer about helping others and what a great honor it would be. What do you think, Drake?"

"She's got moxie," he said. "I like her too."

The liaison was obviously relieved. "I have the paperwork here, if you are ready," she said.

"It's up to Mari, too," Alyssa said. "Are you in?"

"I'm in," Mari replied.

The rest of the meeting was signing documents and setting an appointment for the insertion. Mari agreed to a scheduled C-section so Alyssa and her husband could be there for the birth. Drake suggested daily water aerobics for low impact exercise. Alyssa wanted her to listen to classical music and journal the baby's movements. She selected the high-end diet plan. Lots of fresh fruit, vegetables, and lean protein.

Mari was too close to her next menstruation, so the doctor would wait to begin injections to thicken the lining of her uterus. The implantation was scheduled for the next month. Plenty of time to get the embryos released from the storage facility.

When it was time to leave, Alyssa gave Mari a hug. "So what are you going to study in school?"

"I don't know," Mari said. "I was thinking education. So I could go back and teach in the ward, help kids like me who want off BL, but don't know how to do it. I had this teacher, Mr. Pao. He was really encouraging. The first teacher to tell me I had potential, showing me how the farm could change my life. I was thinking I could be like him for other kids."

"She's bringing a tear to my eye," Drake said.

Alyssa gave her another hug. "I think that's a great plan, Mari. I am so glad we are able to help each other out."

"You know," Drake said wistfully, "Patrick and I went to Julie's graduation from nursing school and bought her these adorable scrubs. We *loved* her! I bet Patrick would be more open to a third if Julie were still at the farm."

"You'll talk him into it," Alyssa said reassuringly. "Besides, you handle most of the childcare. One more shouldn't make a difference to him."

"One more college fund makes a difference," Drake corrected. "But honey, let's talk about you. What have you decided about work?"

"I've got a year of paid leave. I don't have to make any decisions until then." She checked her watch. It had a silver band and Mari could see diamonds glittering in the face. "We've got to catch the rail back to town," she said. "I have a meeting."

"Busy busy high-powered mama," Drake teased.

"Not yet," Alyssa said.

"Soon you won't be hiring and firing executives. Soon you'll be singing silly songs and changing poopy diapers."

"Can't wait," she said, punching him gently in the arm. He laughed. "Goodbye Mari," she said. "I'll be back with my husband for the implantation." They left, Drake arguing that they had time to stop for ice cream and Alyssa warning him about love handles.

"I'm late," Mari said, fiddling with her charm bracelet. It was the first time she had voiced the words that had been pounding in her head the last three days.

"What?" Brandy was doing sit-ups on the floor. She had delivered the baby naturally two weeks earlier. No drugs. She said it was faster and easier the second time. After a week of rest and binding her breasts to stop milk from coming in, Brandy was back to serious exercise and chugging nutrient shakes every morning. She was trying to get cleared for another pregnancy as quickly as possible. The minimum wait time was three months, but if the doctors didn't like the blood tests or bone density scans, they'd make you wait longer. The money from Brandy's last surrogacy went to pay off her mother's house after she had fallen behind on payments. Brandy made sure the property was transferred to her name and charged her mother enough rent to cover taxes and maintenance. Not that she would ever kick her out, Brandy confided to Mari. But her mom needed the threat of it to keep making payments and it wasn't like Brandy had a steady source of income.

"I'm late," Mari repeated.

"Your period?"

"Yeah."

"How late?"

"Three days."

"You ever been late before?"

"No."

"Shit." Brandy stopped doing sit-ups. "Victor."

"He's on Gel. It can't be."

"Check his Index."

Mari looked him up. Victor had started working at the shopping center two months ago. He was off BL. Brandy looked over her shoulder.

"That fucker," Brandy said. "Wait here." She came back ten minutes later with a pregnancy test and a cup.

"Where did you get that?"

"Dear Aunt Cassie. Who else? Pee in here," Brandy ordered, giving her the cup.

Mari took the cup into the bathroom. She dipped the little plastic stick inside it. Almost instantly, a dark blue plus sign appeared.

"What's it say?" Brandy asked.

Mari couldn't speak. She came out, holding the stick.

"Oh hell," Brandy said, looking. "OK. No big deal. We'll take care of it."

"No big deal?" Mari had to fight to keep from screaming. "I'm pregnant! The implantation is in three weeks!"

"Look, there are all kinds of drugs out there. I'll talk to Cassie. She'll get you one tomorrow. You take it and the pregnancy is over. It will just be like a late period. No one will ever know."

"I can't have an abortion."

"It's not an abortion," Brandy said. "You barely missed your period."

"I can't kill my baby."

"Look," Brandy reasoned. "You're not killing a baby. There's no heartbeat. Not this early on. The pill just makes you have a period."

"I'm Catholic."

"For fuck's sake," Brandy said. "You're screwing Victor every weekend, violating all kinds of Bible shit and now you're going to get religious?"

"I know," Mari wailed, "but this is the line for me, alright? Having sex with Victor was just, I don't know. Normal. It felt right. But this feels wrong. It's our baby."

"A baby you didn't want to have."

"It's still our baby."

"And you want to raise it with that lying sack?"

"I've been with Victor since I was thirteen. He loves me."

"He loves you so much he fucked up your one shot at getting off BL? I know guys like him, Mari. You're better than him. Knocking you up was the only way he could keep you. That's why he lied to you. He saw how he was losing you. Every day you live in a place like this you guys get farther and farther apart."

"He wasn't losing me."

"Cassie told me you guys fought all the time. He didn't want you here, did he? It threatened his manhood that you were doing better than him. He wanted to keep you down, at his level."

"That's not true."

"He knows you'll dump him as soon as you get a degree, as soon as you see what a real man is like. A man who can take care of you, who takes responsibility."

"You've got one of those real men?" Mari lashed out. "I don't see him."

"Fuck, Mari. Don't make this about me." Brandy said. "I got my shit together. I was with a fuck-up like Victor for too long. Now I'm free, and once I'm done at the farm, you bet I'm going to find a real man. Someone who doesn't deal drugs or whatever illegal shit Victor is into."

"He's not!" Mari protested.

"Bullshit," Brandy said. "How does he come up with the cash to see you so much? You think they're handing out Benjamins like free samples at the mall?"

"It doesn't matter," Mari said. "It's our baby, and we will raise it together."

"You want to scrape by working at the mall while your kid sits in a shitty diaper all day at the only kind of daycare you'll be able to afford? This is a kid that doesn't want to be born. This is the kid that will ruin your life Mari."

"I can't do it," Mari pleaded.

"I won't tell anyone," Brandy said. "Nobody but me and Cassie will ever know you were even pregnant."

"I would know," Mari said. "I would have to live with it."

"Tell me you want this baby."

"What?"

"Tell me you are overjoyed to have Victor's baby. This is something you always dreamed about. You're ready to be a mother. You're ready to take care of a screaming infant."

"Look, I may not want this baby right now," Mari said.

"But yeah, I always did dream of having kids with Victor."

"If you could go back in time, to the night Victor knocked you up, would you still do it? Would you?" Brandy demanded.

Mari deflated. "No," she whispered. "I wouldn't."

"Then let's go back in time. Take the pill. It will be like nothing happened. You'll be in the clear."

"I couldn't live with myself," Mari said. "I couldn't live with myself knowing I killed my baby."

"Fine," Brandy said harshly. "Then you might as well confess first thing in the morning. Cassie will get fired because they'll have to figure out how this happened. They'll shut it down, tighten security. That will all be on you. Then they'll put you out on the street and getting kicked out of here will go on your Index. What kind of life are you gonna have after that?"

JEREMY AND RACHEL

All those folk who never faced hard times. Those folk who don't see that they momma spit them out with a silver spoon up they ass. They don't see how we hustle. Cleaning nights at that big building downtown. Babysitting days for the grandkids while they momma work at the hotel. Trying to find shoes at the Salvation Army when the snow come through the old ones a size too small. They don't see how we worry. How we one step away from Basic Living. They got no job they live with mommy and daddy. They whine about it and done get profiled in the New York Times with they sad sad story. Then they daddy's friend gives them a job. Those poor suffering folk. Never had a hungry day in they lives. Never hustled in they lives. Shit.

Excerpt from Perspectives from Below, Wired Magazine, 3/30/2042.

"What's on the agenda for today?" Grier asked.

Jeremy sat across from him, the remains of Grier's breakfast on the table.

"You have a call at ten on the real estate deal in Nevada.

Lunch with Marty Lawson at the club at noon. A call with your son at two. Tee time at three, followed by drinks. Dinner scheduled at Abruzzi with Mason Kleinfeld at eight."

"Push the call with my son to next week."

"Yes, sir." It was the third time Grier had rescheduled the call. Jeremy heard a ringing in his earpiece. "One moment, sir." Jeremy tapped his ear. "Mr. Grier's office, how may I help you?" He listened. "I'm sorry, he is not available at this time, may I take a message or would you like his voicemail?" Jeremy typed on his tablet. "You are very welcome. Goodbye."

"Who was that?" Grier asked, pouring himself another cup of coffee from the carafe.

"Someone seeking a donation from AlgiPro. I will direct them to corporate giving."

"Good work, Jeremy. In fact, you've been doing a great job all week."

"Thank you, sir."

The job was easier than Jeremy expected, at least so far. A morning debrief while Grier ate breakfast. Then a lot of answering phone calls and scheduling things. He made travel arrangements for the upcoming board meeting, reserving Grier's private jet and notifying the house manager at Grier's brownstone in San Francisco.

Jeremy's suite of rooms included an office with a large window overlooking the grounds. He spent most of the day there. His lunch was delivered by the kitchen. He didn't know how to cook, so he had tried to eat dinner in the staff dining hall but it was too weird. Tyler and Shana acted normal, but everybody else stole sidelong glances and talked soft enough that he knew they were talking about him. He started having dinners delivered too.

Jeremy really didn't like wearing his ear-piece around the

clock, but the Singh Protocol woman had given him a stern lecture on how important it was. Of course she had been right. Three days into the job, Jeremy got a call in the middle of the night. It was Grier's favorite bartender, giving him a heads up that Grier was on his way home, passed out drunk. Jeremy met the car as it arrived and got Grier safely to his room.

Jeremy refilled Grier's coffee cup. "Your call is in ten, sir."

"Do you want to know why I hired you?"

"Sir?"

Grier poured cream into his coffee. "You've got character. That says more about a man than anything else. This whole week, you've shown restraint, just done your job. I like that."

"Thank you, sir."

"How's your sister?"

"They're planning to operate in a few weeks. The tumor is small enough to remove."

"That's great news!" Grier seemed happy for him. Happy enough that Jeremy decided to ask the question that had been bothering him.

"Can I ask you, sir, about Waverley? That wasn't in any of the paperwork I signed."

"That was a gift," Grier said. "Don't protest. I'm an old man, cynical and weary of this world. It takes a lot to warm my heart. You managed to do that."

"I will pay you back, sir."

"No need," Grier said. "Truly."

"It's too much." Jeremy protested.

"Let me put it in perspective for you," Grier said. "To you, thirteen thousand dollars is what it took to save your sister's life. To me, thirteen thousand dollars is a nice dinner with exquisite wine and good friends. Drop it." Grier's voice was curt.

"Yes, sir. Thank you, sir." Jeremy couldn't help but think of all the people raising money on Gift of Life, and how many of them could be helped by a few of Grier's nice dinners.

Jeremy had never been on an airplane before, but he decided it was even better than Grier's convertible. The private jet was like a small living room, with wide leather seats and tables. A nice woman brought them drinks and a hot breakfast. Grier had gone to sleep after draining his Bloody Mary, reclining his chair until it became a bed. Jeremy spent the flight staring out the window at the clouds, catching glimpses of the land underneath. He took a lot of pictures, especially of the descent into San Francisco. The tiny colorful buildings, growing larger. The miniature cars on thin strips of road. Rachel would love it.

They were flying in on Friday even though the board meeting wasn't until Monday. Grier wanted to meet with a bunch of people. It was also Easter weekend, so Grier had invited his daughter and grandchildren to stay with him at his brownstone. This meant Jeremy was relegated a room at a nearby hotel. He didn't mind one bit. It felt freeing to stay farther than a room away from his boss. Grier had also promised he would get some time off to sightsee, though Jeremy wasn't counting on it.

Grier woke up as the jet landed. They had a few hours before his first meeting, but Grier wanted to go straight to the office. Jeremy had arranged for a car service, and a man in livery was waiting for them at the baggage claim. On the drive in, Jeremy surreptitiously took pictures of Golden Gate Bridge as they drove by. When they arrived, Jeremy hauled their luggage into the lobby and asked the receptionist if there was a place they could store it for the day.

Once Grier was ensconced in the main conference room, Jeremy relaxed. He checked his messages, hoping for an update from his mother, but there was none. Rachel's operation was scheduled for today. Jeremy had wanted to be there for everything, but Grier had insisted that Jeremy accompany him to San Francisco.

Grier's colleague arrived with a stocky young woman, clearly his assistant. Jeremy showed them to the conference room. The assistant followed him in, shutting the door behind her. Jeremy went back to the lobby. He was reviewing Grier's calendar for the next week when his phone rang. It was his mother.

"They won't operate!" She sounded frantic.

"Why?" Jeremy demanded. "I worked out a payment plan. Who do I need to call?"

"It's not that," she said. "They did a scan of her head and the doctor saw a bright spot on her skull. He ordered a full body scan. They found spots all over. I don't understand. Her scan two weeks ago was clear. The doctor kept talking about it being futile to go in and get the brain tumor now."

"Futile?" Jeremy's heart jumped in his chest. "What do you mean futile?"

"He said the bone cancer is aggressive."

Jeremy heard a ringing in his earpiece. He sent it to voicemail. "Aggressive how?"

"It's in almost every limb. It's in her pelvis."

"What about chemo? Radiation?" Jeremy's earpiece rang again. He ignored it.

"I asked. He said we could try, but they don't work so well on bone cancer."

"What does he recommend? Is he there? I want to talk to him." Jeremy heard loud tapping heels coming fast down the hallway toward him.

"Jeremy?" The stocky girl was in a conservative suit and sturdy shoes. "Mr. Grier needs you now."

"Why?"

"How should I know? But he's getting angry, so you better get in there." The girl examined Jeremy's face. "Are you alright?"

"I'm fine." Jeremy put his phone to his ear. "Mom, I'll call you in just a minute." He followed the girl down the hallway.

"I found him in the lobby sir," she said. Grier was seated at the head of the table, the girl's boss to his right. They were huddled over a messy pile of paper.

"Where were you?" Grier said irritably. "Why weren't you answering the goddamn phone?"

"Sorry, sir," Jeremy said. "It's a family emergency." Before Jeremy could elaborate, Grier started talking.

"I have one too," Grier said. "What kind of Easter baskets did you order? My daughter just called to tell me she doesn't want any candy in them this year."

Easter was in two days. Jeremy had not ordered anything. He was certain Grier never asked him to do it and there was nothing about it in Grier's profile. "Sir, I have not ordered any Easter baskets, but I will. Do you have a particular place you use?"

Grier looked at Jeremy like he was an idiot. "It's in the fucking file. They should have been ordered weeks ago."

"So sorry sir, I will get to work on it right now." Jeremy went back into the lobby and searched Grier's profile. There was nothing about Easter baskets. He searched the Farley file and got a hit. Myra at Trellis. He called her.

"I'm swamped," Myra said. "There is no way we can make nine Easter baskets and have them delivered by Sunday morning. I'm not even sure I have the materials."

"Mr. Grier will pay double what the baskets usually cost." Jeremy paced up and down the lobby.

"I don't care if he pays triple, I don't have time to do it. Now, if you'll excuse me..."

"Please don't hang up," Jeremy said. "You've got to help me. I'm pretty new to the job. I didn't know he ordered baskets from you every year. He just mentioned it to me two minutes ago."

"He's going to have to find someone else."

"Myra, please," Jeremy asked, trying to keep from sounding desperate. "Could you at least tell me what you put in the baskets so I could make them myself?"

Myra hung up the phone.

"Damn it," Jeremy muttered. His phone rang. "Mom? I can't talk now."

"Rachel's doctor said he could amputate." His mother's voice was unnaturally calm. "Her left arm at the elbow. Both legs. With the spot on her pelvis they would cut out as much as they had to, but it would probably leave her with a colostomy bag for the rest of her life. Which wouldn't be that long. He says even with amputation she has a week or two left, at the most. He says they have the OR reserved already and the cost would be close enough that you could keep the same payment plan."

"Don't let them do anything. Don't make any decisions. I have to take care of something for Mr. Grier right now, but I'll call you as soon as I can."

Jeremy called Myra back. It went to voicemail. He called

six more times and she finally answered. "Stop calling me," she said.

"Mr. Grier has been a good and loyal customer," Jeremy said, hoping he was speaking the truth. "It is very important to him that his grandchildren receive Easter baskets made by Trellis. I understand that you are overwhelmed, but I will assist in any way that I can to make sure it happens. Please."

There was a long pause. "I understand that you're in a difficult position," Myra said, "but there's really nothing I can do at this point." Jeremy heard the little ping of an incoming email. "That's interesting," Myra said. "I just got a request pushing the delivery of ten baskets to Monday."

"Does that mean you can do nine for me?" Jeremy couldn't believe his luck. He would never be able to pay for Rachel's surgery if he lost his job.

"It does," she said. "I'll still need your help with the ones for the younger kids. The baskets that got pushed were corporate. I need some kiddie items. I don't think Mr. Grier wants a toddler to get an assortment of summer sausages and mustards."

"Send me a list and I'll have everything rush delivered." Jeremy gave her his contact information and hung up the phone. He slumped into the nearest chair and exhaled.

"Myra's going to help?" It was the stocky girl, sitting in the chair across from him. Jeremy hadn't noticed her follow him to the lobby.

"It was you?"

She shrugged. "My boss sends Easter baskets to corporate contacts with religious affiliations. He uses Myra too. I picked ten and changed delivery to office instead of home." She grinned.

"That's brilliant," Jeremy said. "I don't know how I can

thank you."

"Take me out to dinner while you're in town," she said.

"Sounds like a plan," Jeremy said. "That is, if Grier's schedule allows it."

"A late dinner works too," she said.

"You're on."

"Good luck with your sister," she said. "I made a donation on her Gift of Life page."

Jeremy felt his chest tighten. He tried to hold them back, but two tears escaped his eyes. Once it started, he couldn't stop. He put his hands over his face and tried to regain control, shaking from the effort. The woman from Singh Protocol said excessive displays of emotion were unprofessional. Grier could call him any minute. He felt a hand on his back.

"It will be OK," the girl said, giving him an awkward pat. "She'll get better. She looks like a fighter."

HENRY

I got plenty of nothin'
Nothin's plenty for me.
Got subsistence no resistance keep it easy breezy.
Livin' large on the BL, BL, BL.
Lackadaise on the BL, BL, BL.
Makin' hay on the BL, BL, BL.
Keep it all on the DL, DL, DL.
Excerpt from Easy Breezy, by Tony Toni, 2040 Billboard Hot 100.

"But it's my birthday!" She was angry, shouting so loudly that he held the phone away from his ear. Henry had a palette in the other hand, large daubs of oil paint in each well. He was standing at his easel, jars of powders, turpentine, and paint clustered on the table next to him.

"We'll celebrate it after the show. I'm working now."

"You care more about your fucking show than you do about me," she said.

It was true, but Henry did not feel the need to confirm it.

"Say something!" the girl cried.

"We already made plans for next weekend. I don't understand why you're upset."

"If you don't put down that paintbrush and come over right now, this is over. I mean it, Henry."

"You do what you need to do." Henry ended the call and silenced his phone. He turned back to the canvas, all thoughts of his most likely ex-girlfriend gone. He picked up his brush and went back to work, almost in a trance. He worked in a white tank top and paint-spattered jeans, his feet bare. He paced back and forth, contemplating, leanly muscled and intense.

The show was the start of his career. It would launch him into the New York art world. At least that is what his advisor said. Henry presented a few pieces at the student showcase every semester and they always sold, but this year was different. This year, two days after the showcase, his advisor had gotten a call from the manager of a small gallery, known for featuring up and coming artists. The owner had seen Henry's work and wanted to host a summer exhibit. His advisor said it was very rare for this gallery to offer a show to a student. It had been years since the last one.

Henry worked late into the night. When he got back to his apartment, he didn't notice that the girl's toothbrush was gone and the small drawer she had taken for herself was empty. It wouldn't have mattered to him if he had. Henry's girlfriends were like tissue paper, disposable and replaceable. To Henry, only one woman mattered. Irene.

He finagled invites to the Keller gala each year just in case she was there. Every time he was on the subway or walking down the street, he would search the faces around him. His heart would skip a beat any time he saw a petite woman with dark brown hair. He would walk faster, trying to get a closer look. Then she would turn her head and the profile would be wrong. Or the skin would be pale instead of golden. It was never her, but he never stopped looking.

Muttering to himself, Henry began to paint.

The gallery was packed and frenzied. Henry watched from a corner, a glass of wine in hand. He hadn't been able to smooth things over with the girl, so he was at the exhibit alone. He knew it was going well. He could feel it in the energy of the room, the excited conversations, the manager bustling around putting red "sold" stickers below his paintings, a trail of people following her.

The show sold out in an hour. Latecomers pestered the manager first, asking if anything was left. Then they approached Henry, offering congratulations and probing to find out if he had held back any work. But Henry had given it all. A few promised to be in touch about commissioned pieces. People stayed to admire the paintings, but the buzz died down and the crowd thinned.

He saw her standing in front of the large canvases, four portraits of his mother. It was Irene. She looked exactly as he remembered her. Henry walked right over. "It's you," he said, immediately berating himself for making such an idiotic remark.

"Nice to see you again, Henry," Irene said, giving him a sidelong glance. "I came alone this time," she continued. "Did you?"

"I did."

"Are you done here?"

"I am."

"Then let's go." She led him out to the sidewalk and hailed a cab.

"Where are we going?" Henry asked.

"Does it matter?"

Henry woke up in a king-sized bed with Irene sprawled out next to him. She was asleep and the curve of her hip make Henry's fingers itch for a brush. He contented himself with lightly tracing her shape with his index finger. When he got to her waist, Irene shivered and rolled to face him. "Good morning," she said sleepily.

"Good morning." Henry had realized that Irene was older than he first thought the minute she brought him to her apartment. It was too sophisticated. Too established. It wasn't the apartment of a young woman, embarking on a career. Looking at her in the morning light, he tried to guess her age. Her skin was flawless and supple, every part of her taut and smooth. His only clue was in the faint wrinkle lines in her neck.

Irene stretched and cuddled against his chest. "That was fun, Henry. We should do it more often."

"I'm all yours," he said.

"Are you?" she asked.

"If you want me to be."

"I'd like to take you up on that offer." Irene got out of bed and put on a teal silk robe. "Come with me?"

Intrigued, Henry pulled on his boxers and followed her. Irene stopped in front of a pair of large double doors and tugged them open. She stood to one side and let him in. It was an enormous studio, an empty canvas waiting on an easel. Two of the walls were floor to ceiling windows, offering a breathtaking view of the city. The other two walls held paintings. Henry's paintings. Every single one he had sold since starting at Keller.

"I don't understand," Henry said.

"I'm an art dealer," Irene replied. "I took up the profession after my husband, Robert Morris, passed away. He had a few galleries around town. I studied art history in college and got an internship at one of his galleries. That's how we met."

"You bought my art," Henry said, his head spinning.

"I liked it," she said, pausing. "No, that isn't quite true. I loved it. I love it. You're going to have a career, Henry."

"That night," he said. "The night we met."

"I was with someone else."

"Your husband."

"No," she said. "He died a long time ago. It was my last protégé. He's in Paris now."

"Protégé." Henry rolled the word around his mouth. "That's what you want me to be?"

"Yes," she said. "You need a patron, Henry. A place where you are free to work as much as you want, unlimited materials. You need someone to talk about you to the right people. To get your art in front of the right eyes. To set you up with shows at the right galleries."

"Last night was you."

"It was," she admitted. "You were ready. This is just the beginning Henry."

"Did you buy all my art last night, too?" Henry felt vaguely cheated.

"No. Only the four of your mother. They needed to be kept together. But I have cornered the market on the early works of Henry Conell." Irene lifted a large portfolio to the table and slowly flipped through it. She had all of the drawings he had done at the ward, carefully mounted on acid-free boards.

"Where did you get these?"

"Your mother's friend, Mike," she said. "I've been buying them up over the years. Mr. Bautista won't sell, though. Smart man."

"Why?" Henry asked. "What do you get out of this?"

"Well, let's see." Irene stepped out of her robe and draped herself over a white couch. "I get to help a young artist establish himself. I make a commission on his sales. And I get a portrait." She nodded at the empty canvas.

"You also get fucked," Henry said, deliberately crude.

"Usually," she said, laughing. "You didn't seem to mind that part, if I recall correctly."

"Last night I didn't know this was a business deal."

"This is much more than business," Irene said. "I felt it when we met. Didn't you?"

"What about your last protégé?"

"He doesn't need me anymore. You do."

Henry looked at the brand new brushes and unopened bottles of paint. "I need to think about this," he said.

"Certainly," she said. "Want to think about it over here?"

"Damn," Scott said.

"Yeah," Henry said.

"That's hot."

"Yeah."

"How old is she?"

"Thirty-eight."

"Henry's got himself a sugar mama!" Scott teased. "So how does it work? Are you moving in with her?"

"Man, I don't know if I'm saying yes. It doesn't feel right."

"The dream girl you've been pining for is an incredibly

sexy and fabulously rich art dealer who wants to make you famous," Scott said. "What's wrong with that?"

"A lot of things. It's too easy. It's too fast. I feel like I should be working my way up."

"Nobody gets where they are without having someone help them or pull strings," Scott said. "You want to know how I got this internship? My stepdad went to business school with the head of Peace Out San Francisco. She's the one who got my name to the top of the wait list. That's how life works."

"Did you have to sleep with her?"

"Come on, Henry. Irene's not making you sleep with her."

"You know what my mom used to do," Henry said. "This feels like the same thing."

"It's not the same at all, Henry. Is she making you sign a contract? Are you getting paid per fuck?"

"Geez, Scott. She said we would only have sex as long as both of us wanted it."

"Then I see it as a mutually beneficial arrangement between two consenting adults. She clearly likes your art. Just tell her you don't want to sleep with her."

"But I do."

"Then what's the problem?"

"What happens if I don't want to anymore?"

"Then you tell her."

"That's the part I'm worried about."

"Don't overthink this Henry. How long has she given you to decide?"

"Two weeks. She even gave me a list of her past protégés. There are four of them. Said I should call them."

"Are you going to?"

"I haven't decided yet. It's all too much to process. The

show was amazing. Electric. And then seeing Irene again was almost too much. I feel drained. I don't know what to do."

"You need to get away," Scott said. "Look, some of us are going to Vegas next weekend. We have two hotel rooms. One more person isn't going to make a difference. You can sleep on the couch in my room."

"How's your girl going to feel about that?"

"Anna won't care. She's heard all about you. She'll understand."

The waitress brought a tray of shots to the table and unloaded them.

"What are these?" Henry shouted over the music.

"Kamikazes," Anna shouted back, handing one to him. Scott took the third one and they toasted. "Salud!" Anna said, raising the glass.

Henry tossed it back, the vodka burning its way down his throat. He could see why Scott liked Anna. She was gorgeous, with a wavy black mane of hair and luminous brown eyes. She was also a lot of fun to be around.

They each downed two more shots. Anna got up and swayed her hips. She beckoned to Scott.

"You OK?" Scott asked.

"I'm fine," Henry said.

"You sure? You need another drink?"

Henry held up a half-empty highball. "I'm good."

Anna rolled her eyes and reached out to both of them. "Come on guys! Let's dance!"

She pulled them onto the dance floor and sandwiched herself between them. Anna put Henry's hands on her hips, then wrapped her arms around Scott's neck. The three swayed together through several songs. Henry was drunk enough that the whole experience was surreal. The pulsating music, the dimly lit room, the colored lights flashing. They were joined by a few more interns Henry recognized from dinner. One of the girls pressed herself against Henry. He turned around. She was blonde and curvy, wearing a backless halter top and no bra.

"You're Scott's friend. The artist, right?" she shouted.

"Henry," he said. He danced with the blonde for two more songs, then excused himself to use the bathroom. When he got back, Anna and Scott were back at the table, Anna chatting with the blonde.

"Body shots!" Anna said as Henry approached. She was holding a salt shaker and a lime. Scott licked Anna's neck and sprinkled salt on it. He licked again and downed the shot while Anna put the lime into her mouth. Scott took it from her, lingering to kiss her. "Your turn, Henry!" Anna said.

The blonde offered her cleavage, but Henry licked her neck instead. They all went back on the dance floor and the blonde continued to flirt with Henry. He was tempted, but he couldn't shake the thought of Irene, her exotic beauty nothing like this corn-fed all-American girl.

"Want to come back to my room?" the blonde offered.

"I have a girlfriend," Henry said. It was sort of true.

"That's too bad," the blonde said. She finished out the song with him and turned her attention back to one of the other interns.

"What happened?" Anna asked, stepping in to take the blonde's place. "She liked you."

Henry shrugged. "Where's Scott?" he asked.

"Bathroom. I think that last shot messed him up."

"I should go check on him."

"OK," Anna danced over to the blonde, clearly going to get an answer to her question. The girls danced closely, the guys watching and cheering them on.

Henry found Scott bent in half and vomiting into a toilet. "This is familiar," Henry said.

"Fuck you," Scott croaked. He vomited again.

Henry got some paper towels and dampened them.

"Thanks," Scott said, wiping his mouth and spitting. He went to the sink and rinsed.

"Better?" Henry asked.

"Yeah," Scott said. "I think I'm going to call it a night."

"Me too," Henry said.

Anna reluctantly came back with them to the room and went into the bedroom with Scott. Henry stripped down to his boxers and turned on the television. He was flipping through channels when Anna came out wearing a huge t-shirt. She sat down next to him and put her feet up on the coffee table.

"Scott passed out," she said. "I made him drink a big glass of water and take some hangover pills."

"You guys are good together," Henry said. "He really likes you."

"I really like him," Anna said. "He's a good guy."

"He is," Henry said. "We've been friends a long time."

"I know," Anna said. "From when he was on BL, right?"

"Yeah."

"He told me what's been going on with you," Anna said. "I hope that's OK."

"I figured he would," Henry said. "So what do you think?"

"I think you should say yes," Anna said promptly. "From what Scott's told me, life on BL sucks. Art isn't exactly lucrative. If Irene can make it happen for you, then do it."

"Did Scott mention the part about sleeping with her?"

"Yes," Anna said. "I don't see anything wrong with it."

"Aren't you Christian?" Scott had told Henry all about Anna's weird virgin thing. She drew the line at sex, but didn't mind everything leading up to it.

"Yeah, but you aren't. So the rules don't really apply to you."

"I've never heard a Christian talk like that before."

"Look, it's pretty simple. As it stands, you're going to hell anyway, right? Sucks, but it's true. So it's not like you doing this thing with Irene is going to change that. And if you become a Christian at some later point in life, you'll be forgiven for all your past sins, so you're cool."

"How drunk are you?" Henry asked.

"I'm serious," Anna said.

"Shouldn't you be trying to convert me? Get some brownie points?"

"No such thing where God is concerned," Anna said. "I can't turn you into a Christian anymore than I can turn this coffee table into a dog. Only God can do it."

"So Christian virgin Anna is telling me I should fuck Irene in exchange for a career in art?"

"It's kind of like marriage, isn't it?"

"It's not like marriage at all, Anna."

"It totally is," Anna said, giggling. "Like, I'll fuck my husband and take care of the kids and he'll go to work and make the money. It's a business deal. Just like what Irene offered you, without the marriage part."

"That's pretty cold, Anna."

"You have to be logical about marriage if you want it to work."

"What about love?"

Anna laughed. "Henry the romantic! Love is a huge part of it. I'd never get married if I didn't love the guy. But it's not like love always stays passionate and shiny. Marriage is a commitment to stick it out, right? Good times and bad? Or at least that is what it is supposed to be. These days a lot of people don't. How many people choose contractual marriage and end it if anything goes wrong? How is that any different from what Irene wants?"

"It feels different. It feels like selling myself."

"It's not selling yourself if you want it. She's supposedly a knockout and you clearly have the hots for her if you passed up a chance to hook up with Isla." Noting Henry's questioning look, she clarified. "The cute blonde."

"She wasn't my type," Henry said.

"Liar," Anna said. "Isla is everyone's type. But whatever, Henry. In the end, you have to do what lets you sleep at night."

"Do you sleep at night?"

"Like a baby." Anna yawned. "This is your fork in the road, Henry. That huge decision you're going to look back on when you're 40 and think, that's where everything changed." Anna shook her head. "I'm getting maudlin."

"Why? What's going on with you?"

"I'm going to turn down my offer. All I ever wanted was to work for Peace Out. It's where the best of the best go and I like being the best. But doing it for real is so different than what I thought it would be like. Death sucks, Henry. People suck. I can't really talk about it because of the non-disclosure, but some crazy stuff went down. I can't stop thinking about it. It's too much. Like what if things had gone the other way, you know?"

Henry didn't really know, but he nodded.

"It's my huge decision, changing the course of my life. Just like you, right?" Anna yawned again and looked back toward the bedroom. "I'm tired. See you in the morning, Henry."

"Good night, Anna." Henry stayed up, brooding, until the sunlight replaced the neon glow coming through the windows.

When Henry got back to New York, he went straight to Irene's apartment. It was past midnight, but she was still awake and told the doorman to send him up. She answered the door wearing the same silk robe she had worn after their first night together.

"Will you marry me?" Henry asked without preamble.

Irene laughed and pressed one hand to her heart. "Henry, this is so sudden!"

"I'm serious, Irene," Henry said. "I've thought about your offer and I want to accept it. But only if you'll marry me."

"Why don't you come in and we can talk about it?" Irene opened the door wide to let Henry past her. "I'll pour us some wine." Irene took the cork out of a half-empty bottle of cabernet and poured two glasses. Handing one to Henry, she sat on a barstool at the counter. "Henry, why do we have to define what we have together?"

"It has to be defined at some point," Henry said. "We'll have a business agreement with my art. I want something personal to go with it. I need it."

Irene swirled the wine in her glass, watching Henry with calm regard.

"You know a lot about me. You know about my mother and Mike. Do you understand why I can't do what you want?"

"Do I look like a pimp, Henry?" Irene asked.

"Of course not," Henry said. "But it doesn't matter. I'd still feel like a prostitute."

"So marrying me makes it all better?"

"I would have stayed with you," Henry said. "Without your offer." He opened up his wallet and took out a battered, folded piece of paper and gave it to Irene. She opened it slowly. It was the sketch Henry had made of her. "I drew that the night we met," Henry said. "I've carried it with me for years. Seeing you at my show was like the missing part of my life had finally appeared. Then to find out that you've been thinking of me as much as I've been thinking of you... What we have is special, Irene. Please, marry me."

Irene pondered the sketch for a long while, so long Henry started to lose hope. Finally, she spoke. "Marrying me would impact your career in a negative way. If we have a public relationship, then anything I do to promote you could be seen as nepotism."

"You had relationships with your other protégés."

"Nothing Indexed."

"Do you believe in my art? In me as an artist?"

"Yes," Irene said without hesitation.

"Then I don't care what anyone else thinks. Actors marry their directors. Musicians marry their managers." Henry stepped closer to Irene, putting his wine on the counter and sliding his hands around her waist. "I want you, Irene. I want this."

Irene put her own glass down. She placed her palm against Henry's cheek. "I'll agree to a one year contract with mutual option to renew, including a pre-nup. Will that suffice?"

"Yes," Henry said.

Irene drew his face toward hers.

VERA AND BOB

The poor don't have a safety net. They don't have a network of people who can help when the unexpected happens. They don't have savings accounts or 401ks and IRAs to borrow against. All it takes is for one thing to go wrong and they end up on Basic Living. Pay the rent or buy food. See the doctor for that nasty cough or pay the electricity bill. And when all those unpaid bills catch up to them, they drop onto Basic Living.

Sucks to be them, right? Aren't you glad you aren't them?

Excerpt from Nolan Barber: The Shadow of Basic Living, TED Talk, posted 3/26/2045.

"Should we pack our bags?" Vera asked.

"I think so," Bob replied. "We should probably be ready to go as soon as we tell them."

They packed in silence, Bob folding clothes while Vera gathered up everything they had stashed over the week. There were a dozen small jars of jam from breakfast and a plastic bag full of sugar packets and tea bags.

"Don't forget the shampoo," Bob said.

"I didn't." Vera put two lotion bottles into her backpack and zipped it up. "I wish we didn't have to go."

"We'll be back next year," Bob assured her. "Want to try New Orleans?"

"What about Chicago?" Vera figured planning the next trip would be half of the fun. Something to look forward to, something to keep Bob's spirits up. She could probably drag out the decision over which city to visit through Christmas.

There was a knock on the door. It was their Facilitator. "Hi Vera," he said. "Are you and Bob ready? I'm here to escort you to the Peace Room."

"Well," Vera said, shifting her weight from one foot to the other. "We've changed our minds. We don't want to Peace Out."

"That's right," Bob said, coming to stand behind her. "Facilitation has shown us we still have living left to do."

"I understand," the Facilitator said with no change of expression, as if it happened all the time. Vera wondered if maybe it did. "Why don't you come with me to my office and we'll process you out."

"Should we bring our bags?" Vera asked.

"If they're already packed," the Facilitator said.

After a short walk, they were back where they had started just a week before, sitting in the Facilitator's office with their backpacks at their feet. The Facilitator asked them to repeat their decision against Peacing Out and asked for their reasons, so that Peace Out could improve the Facilitation process. Vera felt mildly guilty about it all, and let Bob do most of the talking.

"Well, that's it," the Facilitator said. "But I wanted to let you know that Peace Out instituted a new policy just last month. We only allow people to go through Facilitation twice.

After that, you are no longer welcome at Peace Out. We've had an uptick in individuals using Peace Out for selfish reasons, undermining the solemnity and purpose of our organization." The Facilitator's tone was not accusatory in any way, but Vera felt like a school-child being reprimanded.

"That's terrible," Bob said smoothly. "Our youngest son Peaced Out in Nashville and we very much appreciate what you do for everyone."

"Have a safe trip back to Nashville," the Facilitator said, rising to see them out.

"Thank you," Vera said. "This week here has meant so much to both of us."

Bob and Vera were quiet on most of the train ride home. About fifty miles from Nashville, Bob broke the silence. "I guess too many people were doing what we did."

"I guess so," Vera said.

"There goes our vacation."

"I'm glad they changed the rules," Vera declared. "I never felt more ashamed than when that Facilitator said what he did about us being selfish."

"He wasn't talking to us," Bob said.

"Yes, he was. He was talking about people like us," Vera said. "It's the same thing. And how you came back at him, cool as a cucumber, talking about Charlie. It wasn't right."

"What I said was true."

"Not true enough to keep us from doing what we did," Vera said.

"You had a good time, Vera. Best time you've had in years. Don't try to deny it."

"I'm not denying it, I'm just saying, I don't feel so good about it anymore."

"That Facilitator is making six figures a year and sitting pretty. He has no idea how we live. He couldn't do it for a day, let alone a decade. We tried our best, didn't we? We did everything we could to make a living. I took any job that would have me, didn't I? We counted pennies trying to keep off BL. The system is rigged, Vera. We just took something back. Something for ourselves. What's so wrong with that?" Bob got that petulant look Vera had seen on every one of their children's faces.

"Well, it's all over and done with now," she said. "No use talking about it. I had a nice time with you, make no mistake about that."

"You took a wrong turn there, Jolene," Bob called from the backseat.

"No, I didn't." Jolene looked at him through the rearview mirror. "Don't you two want to come over for dinner? Tell us all about your trip?"

"Of course," Vera said. "I've missed that little baby girl, too. How is she?"

"She was napping when I left," Jolene said. "I'm guessing Chris is giving her a bottle right about now."

When they got to Jolene's house, she parked in the driveway and they all got out. "I want to show you something," Jolene said. She took them through the side door of the garage and turned on the light. There was drywall up on one wall and a full-size bed and box springs against it, mismatched lamps on bedside tables with drawers on either side. There was a faded rug on the concrete floor and a stack of boxes against another wall. "It's still a work-in-progress," Jolene said. "But Chris and I think it will do nicely."

"Is this for us?" Vera asked.

"It is," Jolene said. "If that's what you want... Mom, are you OK?"

"I just need to sit down for a minute." Vera sank onto the bed.

"I got a call from your Facilitator on your third day there," Jolene said. "He didn't say a word about what you all were doing, but he had to have known. He said that just in case you decided not to Peace Out, I should know about this new program the government is trying out. It's called Intergen. See, it's cheaper for them if you aren't on BL, so they give us a stipend to have you live with us. I talked with Chris about it, and he saw how much help you were, Mom and he knows what a hard worker you are, Dad.

"The stipend isn't a lot, but if you guys get jobs like Mom mentioned to cover extra costs, then we should be able to save all of it toward a down payment on a house of our own in a few years, one big enough for you to have a real room. And when you can't work anymore, we'll use the stipend to care for you until you guys are ready to Peace Out."

"Jolene," Bob choked up and cleared his throat. He tried to speak again, but couldn't get the words out. He gave his daughter a bear hug.

"I'll say it for both of us," Vera said. "Thank you."

"You thank that Facilitator," Jolene said. "I'd never have known how to get in that program without him."

MARI AND VICTOR

"Tonight we have with us Sonics forward and all-star Terrence Howell, reading our Top Ten Reasons to go on Basic Living. Go ahead, Terrence!"

"10. Never worry about paying bills again.

"9. Make a fashion statement with BL Greys.

"8. BL has a 0% unemployment rate!

"7. Those new BL wards look really nice.

"6. Where else can you get free birth control?

"5. Who wouldn't want government healthcare?

"4. It looks really good on your Index.

"3. Toughen up your namby pamby little kids.

"2. The AlgiPro diet is a surefire way to lose those holiday pounds!"

"And now, Terrence, what's the number one reason to go on Basic Living?"

"1. Know without doubt she isn't with you because of your money!"

Late Night Top Ten with Andrew Pearson, 1/4/36.

"I wanted to tell you in person," Mari said.

"I appreciate that," Cassie replied. Her back was to Mari and she was pouring lemonade. It was uncomfortably hot in her apartment. Cassie had apologized for the broken air conditioner. She put a straw in each glass and carried over a tray with the drinks and some sugar cookies. Cassie handed a glass to Mari and settled into her Barcalounger. "So you're pregnant."

"I am. I've decided to have the baby."

Cassie didn't say anything at first. She just stirred her lemonade. Without looking up, she spoke. "There are other options."

"Abortion is not an option."

"Brandy mentioned that," Cassie said. "I'm not suggesting that. But we can salvage this situation. I could set up an embryo transfer. We can say you have a family emergency and get a few days leave. I'll escort you. We get you a surrogate at a cheaper farm, maybe in Arizona. Once the kid is born you put him up for adoption or ship him to your mom while you get your degree. Nobody has to know."

"That sounds expensive," Mari said.

"I'll loan you the money and you can pay me back out of your surrogate fees," Cassie said. "My job is on the line here."

"I would never tell them about you." Mari felt the sweat beading on her forehead and gulped down some lemonade.

"I know, dear," Cassie said, offering her a cookie. "But they'd find out eventually. An embryo transfer would be better for all of us. Give me three days. I just have to make a few calls and take some money out of my retirement. We can have it done next week. You'll have plenty of time to recover before the implantation."

"Are you sure about this?" Mari asked. She wasn't hungry,

but took a bite of cookie to be polite, washing it down another long drink.

Cassie nodded.

"I don't know how to thank you," Mari said, barely able to hold back tears. "I couldn't sleep all night thinking about how much I screwed up."

"From what Brandy told me, it's Victor who screwed up. Have you talked to him?"

"Not yet," Mari said, sniffling. "I don't understand why he did this to me."

"He probably wasn't thinking at all," Cassie said. "Don't worry, Mari. Everything is going to be OK. Just act like everything is normal and we'll talk soon."

Mari spent the rest of the afternoon in her room, trying to do practice questions for her college placement exam. After three hours, she had only gotten through five questions. She had dinner in the cafeteria with Brandy, but they kept the conversation to innocuous topics like the handsome new masseuse. Back in the room, Brandy shut the door and leaned back against it.

"OK, the suspense is killing me. What did Cassie say?"

"She offered to set up an embryo transfer. Make it so I can stay."

"No way!" Brandy exclaimed. "That's insane."

"Your aunt is awesome."

"Well, she's covering her own ass. It's not out of the goodness of her heart."

"I get that," Mari said. "But I'm still so grateful. I could never afford an embryo transfer or surrogate on my own."

"Are you going to keep the baby?"

"I haven't decided yet," Mari admitted. "But I've got

time."

Mari opened her eyes. It was still dark out and she could hear Brandy snoring softly. Her body felt strange and heavy. She felt dampness under her, as if she had wet the bed. Mari felt around with one hand. In the moonlight she could see darkness staining her palm. She turned on her bedside lamp. Brandy groaned and rolled away from the light. Mari's fingers were red. So was the switch to the lamp. Mari pulled back her sheets to see the spread of blood beneath her.

"Brandy!" Mari cried, her breath coming faster and faster.

Brandy sat straight up. "What the hell?" she demanded. Mari just whimpered and Brandy saw the sheets. "Holy shit. I'll call Cassie. Go change. I'll strip the bed."

Mari stumbled to the bathroom. Her underwear was soaked as was the bottom of her shirt. She put the clothes in the sink and took a brief shower. The water flowing down her legs made a dark pink swirl around the drain. Brandy knocked on the door and put a clean set of clothes on the counter.

"Cassie wants to know if you're still bleeding."

"Yes, but not a lot," Mari said.

"OK. That's good," Brandy said. "She says to use a pad, not a tampon."

Mari got dressed and rolled her bloody clothes into a ball, the cleanest part of her shirt on the outside. She threw it on top of the pile of bedclothes in the middle of the room. "I lost the baby," Mari said. "That was the baby."

Brandy didn't say anything.

"I prayed for it to happen," Mari whispered. "Ever since the pregnancy test. When Cassie offered me the embryo transfer I thought it was a miracle. A way to keep the baby and my future. But God answered my prayer instead."

"It doesn't work like that," Brandy said, her voice quiet.

"It just did."

They heard a soft knock on the door. It was Cassie, holding a fresh set of sheets and a black garbage bag. "I'm sorry," she said to Mari, shaking out the garbage bag.

"It wasn't your fault," Mari said.

Cassie hesitated for a second before stuffing the dirty pile into the bag. "I'm still sorry." Brandy was helping Cassie make the bed when Mari moaned, doubling over.

"Are you OK?" Brandy asked.

"I don't know," Mari said. She winced again and pressed a hand to her abdomen.

"Cramping is normal," Cassie said. She took a bottle of pills out of her pocket and gave it to Mari. "This is just Tylenol. It's approved so you don't have to worry about the drug screening. Take two of these every four hours until it stops. You'll be fine in a day or two."

Mari waited at the table, set for three. The implantation was in two hours, but Alyssa had scheduled a lunch with Mari first. She wanted her husband to meet the surrogate, even though it was really too late for them to change their minds. The paperwork was signed, the embryo was defrosted and Mari was prepped. She was fully recovered from her miscarriage. Cassie had been right, the bleeding stopped within a few days. When Mari went in for injections the next week, the doctor did a full examination. If he could tell, he didn't say a word.

After consulting with Brandy, Mari decided not to tell Victor about the pregnancy. But she did confront him about being off BL when he called to schedule another tryst. With Brandy sitting right next to her for moral support, Mari finally told Victor she needed a break. She took his name off the visitor list and blocked his calls. When he started calling her from other phones she changed her number. Brandy said Mari didn't need the stress in her life, that it wouldn't be good for the baby. She made Mari join her for yoga every morning.

Mari poured herself more water from the carafe on the table. She was getting hungry and hoped that the clients would arrive soon. There was a basket of bread on the table, but she thought it would be rude to start without them. When Alyssa breezed in a few minutes later, she was alone. Mari stood to greet her.

"Sorry I'm late," Alyssa said. "My husband had a last minute work emergency." She rolled her eyes. "I didn't want to postpone the implantation. Who knows what his schedule will be like? He can meet you some other time. We'll have at least nine months." Alyssa sat down.

A waiter came by, took their orders, and cleared away the third place setting. The farm maintained a small restaurant for clients and potential clients, open only for breakfast and lunch. The girls normally ate in the cafeteria and served themselves. The clients could get a tour of the cafeteria if they wanted, but it was far more utilitarian than the small tables set with white linen.

"So I saw that you and Victor are no longer together," Alyssa said. "What happened?"

"Once you picked me, he couldn't handle it," Mari said. "He didn't like thinking about me carrying someone else's baby."

"It's how a lot of people do it these days," Alyssa said. "I had eggs frozen when I was eighteen. It was my high school graduation present. The best gift they could have given me." Alyssa noticed Mari's confused expression. "It set me free of my biological clock," she explained. "I didn't feel any pressure to settle with an unsuitable mate just to have babies. I didn't have to put the brakes on my career to deal with pregnancy and caring for an infant. And now Sean and I have the financial security and emotional stability to provide for our children."

"I'm sorry," Mari said. "It's just, where I'm from, that's not how it happens."

"Oh I know," Alyssa said. "The problem is Gel."

"What do you mean?"

"Getting off Gel and getting off BL have become synonymous in BL culture. It's really bad. They need to do more education in the wards, show people that they should stay on Gel until they are ready to have babies."

"I think people are really worried about staying off BL," Mari said. "If they don't have babies while they are off, they could never have them."

"That's just the wrong way of thinking," Alyssa said. "What puts you on BL is having a baby when you aren't ready to take care of it. Sean and I have been on Gel since we were fourteen."

"Really? I thought only people on BL had to be on Gel."

"It's not required, but it's like getting vaccinated," Alyssa said. "Everyone does it because it's stupid not to. I mean, there are always people on the fringes who refuse, but why? Why take the chance on your teenager doing something dumb and coming home pregnant?"

"What would you do if that happened?" Mari asked tentatively.

"Terminate," Alyssa said. "It's the easiest answer."

"What about embryo transfer?"

"Way too invasive," Alyssa said dismissively. "It's

basically a c-section." She looked around for the waiter. "Are they harvesting the lettuce for our salads?" Alyssa laughed at her own joke, stopping when she saw Mari's face. "Are you OK? You look a little pale."

"I'm fine," Mari said faintly. "Maybe if I eat something?" She reached for the bread basket and buttered a slice, her hands trembling.

"Are you sick?" Alyssa asked. "I don't want to do the implantation if you're sick."

"No, I'm really OK," Mari protested. "I just haven't eaten since breakfast." She quickly finished the slice of bread. "I feel much better already."

"I'm going to talk to the doctor about your blood sugar," Alyssa said.

JEREMY AND RACHEL

You don't know me.
You wonder why a girl on BL wears designer jeans.
You think dark thoughts about how I got them.
You hoped BL would show us our place.
You thought we would finally learn we are less than you.
You wanted us to know it in our BL greys, but
You don't know Minerva P. Young. And so...
You seethe over her fancy cast-offs, worn by her brown first cousin.
You don't know me.

"Minerva P. Young" by Serena Solomon, sophomore at The Keller School of Chicago, 2052.

"Sorry it's so late, Mom. I can talk now." Jeremy closed the door to his hotel room and started changing out of his work clothes. Grier had kept him in meetings until he and the stocky assistant's boss decided to go for steaks and scotch.

Jeremy had finally learned her name. It was Paige and he

was meeting her for dinner in an hour. Both of them were free and neither knew when or if it would happen again while Jeremy was in San Francisco. Paige had tried to let him off the hook when she learned how serious things were with Rachel, but Jeremy had insisted. He zipped up his jeans and carefully hung up his coat and pants. "Mom, can you hear me?" Jeremy asked.

"I'm here." His mother's voice was rough.

"I've got it all figured out," Jeremy said. "First thing in the morning, you are going to talk to Rachel's doctor and insist they start radiation and chemo. I'm going to research every bone cancer drug trial in the country and get her into a program."

"No," his mother replied. "I'm taking Rachel to Peace Out."

"No!" Jeremy shouted. "You can't!"

"I'm her mother," she said, her voice cracking. "I have to do what's best for her."

"That isn't what's best for her, Mom. Rachel deserves a chance to fight."

"Don't you understand? There is no chance. There is no hope. My baby girl is going to die no matter what we do."

"Please, Mom. Don't do this."

"It's already done. We have an appointment for tomorrow. She's considered high priority so there's no waiting period."

"There has to be another way," Jeremy pleaded. "You can't just Peace her Out!"

"Do you want them to poison her first? Do you want them to cut her to pieces? Because that's all they can offer. She hurts, Jeremy. She hurts so much and it's getting worse by the hour. The standard painkillers don't work. The doctor just got approval to give her bliss."

"You let them?"

"You weren't here. You didn't see her screaming, begging me to make it stop."

"How is she now?"

"Asleep, finally." His mother let out a ragged breath. "You've done all that you can, Jeremy. You gave us three more months with her. We were blessed to have that. But it's time to let her go."

"Does she know? Have you told her?"

"I told her we are going to a place that will make the pain stop forever. I told her she will be healed and have a perfect body in heaven. She asked if she could wear the dress you gave her."

"Don't do this without me. Postpone it. Wait until I get home."

"The doctor said we were lucky to get a slot this quickly. I'm not giving it up. I'm not letting my child live with this kind of pain any longer than I have to. Come home now. Be here for both of us. She would want it that way."

"I'll be there," Jeremy said. "I will definitely be there."

Jeremy took a cab to the restaurant where Grier and his companion were having dinner. They were seated in a private room, surrounded by racks of wine behind glass walls. Jeremy knocked before entering.

"So sorry to interrupt, Mr. Grier, but may I speak with you for a moment?"

"What is it, Jeremy?" Grier took a puff of his cigar.

Jeremy briefly explained his sister's condition and his mother's plan. "I would like permission to fly back to Atlanta tonight."

"To say goodbye," Grier nodded. "I understand."

"No, sir." Jeremy said. "I want to get guardianship of my sister. I need to stop my mom from doing this."

"You've got no grounds, son," Grier's companion said. "No judge would grant you that request, not with what you've told us. If they're giving her bliss..." The old man shook his head, Grier murmuring in agreement.

"I have to try."

"Sometimes we have to let go," Grier said abruptly. "We have to stop trying."

"Begging your pardon, but if it was your wife, sir," Jeremy began.

"It *was* my wife," Grier interrupted, his voice growing harsh. Grier's companion averted his eyes. "It was cancer that took her, too. She was bedridden at the end. High on as many drugs as they could pump into her. Lucid for a few minutes a day if I was lucky and how I treasured those minutes. Until she begged me to let her die. Begged for days, and I couldn't do it. Then I had a meeting downtown. Unavoidable if I wanted to keep control of the company. My wife managed to turn up the drip rate on all her IVs. She was brain dead when I got home." Grier emptied his tumbler of scotch in one swallow. "Peace Out finished what she started. I never got to say goodbye. Don't make the same mistake. Don't fight the inevitable. You go home and you tell Rachel how much you love her. And then you let her go." Grier spoke with a finality that brooked no arguing.

"Yes sir." Jeremy said. "When do you need me back?"

"Monday morning for the board meeting," Grier said promptly. "Expense the travel."

"Thank you, sir," Jeremy said.

Grier's companion spoke up. "Dan, I'll give you my

assistant's number. She can help out over the weekend."

"Perfect," Grier said. "One thing before you go, Jeremy, are the Easter baskets ordered?"

"OK, I've found eight cancer trials in the greater Atlanta area, but none of them relate to bone cancer. One is taking people with a terminal prognosis," Paige looked up from her tablet. She was lying on her stomach on the bed. Jeremy was kneeling on the floor, packing.

"Can you enlarge the geography of the search?" Jeremy asked.

"Already did," Paige said. "The only bone cancer trials accepting patients are in Minnesota and Arizona."

"Can you send me the info on those and the terminal one?"

"Sending right now," Paige said. "What about you?"

"I filed an online form for a temporary restraining order with the court in Atlanta. It doesn't open until Monday, but if I give the completed form to the people at Peace Out it should stop them."

"Are you sure?" Paige sounded doubtful.

"They can't Peace Out Rachel until a court decides who her guardian should be. My mom is on BL and I'm not. I should be able to get guardianship." Jeremy said it with more conviction than he felt. He had read everything he could find on the court's website, but there was nothing relevant to his situation. He also found another site dedicated to helping people stop a loved one from Peacing Out. There was a list of lawyers on one page. Jeremy had emailed them all and was waiting for replies. "I'm sorry, Paige. This isn't the kind of dinner I wanted us to have." Their empty plates were stacked on a tray near the hotel room door. "Thank you for helping me. I really appreciate it."

"You're welcome," Paige said. "Anything I can do, just let me know."

"You can come visit us in Atlanta," Jeremy said. "Rachel and I will take you out for barbecue."

"It's a deal," Paige said. Her phone rang. "Just a minute," she said, picking up and listening. "Yes, sir. I'll be there right away." Paige ended the call. "Duty calls. It looks like Mr. Grier's had a little too much to drink." She stood up and stretched.

"His hangover pills are in the upper left compartment of his toiletries bag," Jeremy said, going to open the door for her. "If he starts cussing, that means he's about to throw up."

"Thanks for the tip," she said dryly. She paused and then gave Jeremy a solid hug. "You're one of the good guys, Jeremy. I'm glad that we met."

"I'm glad we met, too."

She pulled back and looked up at him. "Can you promise me something?"

"What?"

"If things don't work out the way you want them to, promise me that you'll be OK."

"I can't promise that."

"Then promise me that you will always honor your sister by living the kind of life she would want for you."

"That's not a hard promise. She's going to be living that life with me," Jeremy said firmly.

Paige dropped her arms and stepped away. "Goodbye, Jeremy. Your cab will be here in about twenty minutes." Paige stepped into the hall and looked back. "I'll be praying for her to pull through. Let me know how it goes."

HENRY

He grew up on Basic Living. His mother was addicted to bliss. He was addicted to the sky. Based on the true story of the first manned expedition to Mars.

Promotional poster for Ares IX, release date 12/2/2068. Text over image of a young boy with his back to the camera, standing in the middle of a busy crosswalk and looking up as a rocket passes overhead.

"What's the occasion?" The clerk at Tiffany's slid a tray of bracelets out of the glass case and set it in front of Henry.

"Anniversary," Henry said. "Our third." He was keeping the evening low-key since Irene was flying in from the opening of her new gallery in California. Henry would have gone with her, but he was finishing a series of portraits of children in the BL wards. The show was opening in just a few days and the media interest had been enormous. Irene had loved Henry's idea to donate half the proceeds to scholarship funds for the children. The exhibit was already booked for a yearlong tour around the country and ticket sales were strong. With limited edition prints and assorted merchandise for sale, Henry expected the scholarships to be more than enough to pay for his subjects' college educations. Irene had done her job. Henry's original works were selling for upwards of a hundred thousand dollars. He had just inked a deal with Macy's for a mainstream line of home decor.

"Do you like any of these?" The clerk was solicitous.

"Maybe something with emeralds?" Henry asked. "To match her eyes."

The clerk took out a different tray. One in particular caught Henry's eye. It was a cuff bracelet with emeralds and diamonds in geometric settings, an homage to Art Deco. It was perfect. "I'll take this one," he said.

The clerk gently placed the bracelet in a blue box and tied a satin ribbon around it. "Excellent choice, sir," he said.

Back at their apartment, Henry chopped fresh tomatoes, bell peppers, mushrooms, garlic, and onions. He browned some Italian sausage in a pan and put the onions in a pan with olive oil. He was filling a pot with water when his phone rang.

"You made it!" Henry said.

"Just landed," Irene said. "We're still taxiing."

"I'm in the middle of making wild mushroom fettuccini."

"Sounds delicious," she said.

"How was the flight?"

"Blessedly boring."

Henry heard the squawking sounds of a flight attendant talking over the intercom.

"We're pulling up to the gate," Irene said. "See you in a bit."

Henry finished making the sauce and set the stove to simmer. He opened a bottle of Chianti and poured it into a decanter. He cut a half dozen slices of crusty bread and rubbed them with garlic cloves, butter, and a generous sprinkle of Parmesan cheese. Dessert was a small plate of truffles and macarons from Irene's favorite patisserie.

Irene arrived an hour later. Henry greeted her with a kiss, carrying her bag to their room. They enjoyed dinner and a lengthy bath together, after which Henry presented Irene with the bracelet.

"It's lovely," she said, putting it on. "Thank you, Henry."

"Happy Anniversary."

"Happy Anniversary," she echoed. Irene toyed with the bracelet, rotating it around her wrist. "I've got something for you, too," she said. "But we'll have to get dressed, first." She walked into the closet and came out wearing a sundress and ballet flats.

Intrigued, Henry donned a pair of jeans and a black button-down shirt. "Where are we going?"

"You'll see," Irene said.

They took the car to a building in SoHo. Irene nodded at the doorman and took Henry to the top floor. She stopped in front of an ancient door, large with brass fittings. She handed him a key. "Go on," she said.

Henry opened the door. It was a loft, tastefully furnished with huge windows.

"Are we moving?" Henry asked.

"Not quite," Irene said. "It's yours."

"Mine? I don't understand."

"Henry, you don't need me anymore. You are a success. The most successful of my protégés. This is my gift to you."

"What are you talking about, Irene?"

"I'm not renewing our marriage contract, Henry."

"No," Henry said. "You can't."

"I'm letting you go, Henry. I'm setting you free."

"I don't want to be free," Henry said. "I want to be with you."

"You say that now," Irene replied. "I'm almost twenty years older than you."

"That doesn't matter to me."

"It will. I know it will." Irene sighed. "What we have is beautiful and that's how I want to remember it. I want us to be good friends. I want to toast at your wedding and send gifts to your children."

"I love you, Irene. How can I make you understand that? There is no other woman for me."

"You had many women before me, and you will have many woman after."

"Fuck this," Henry said. "Let's get married. For real this time. Permanent contract. No prenup. I want to be with you 'til death do us part."

"That's very sweet, Henry."

"It's not fucking sweet. What is wrong with you? Twenty minutes ago we were heading to bed after celebrating our anniversary and now you're saying it's over?"

Irene looked away. "You know I was never able to have children," she said. "Richard and I tried for years. My protégés are my legacy, Henry. In a way, you are my child. Every child leaves home someday."

"I'm not your fucking child."

"You're acting like one now," Irene said. "We had a contractual marriage for a reason."

"You wanted the contractual marriage."

"We hardly knew each other."

"We know each other now," Henry said. "I know your heart, Irene. You love me. I know you're afraid of getting hurt, but I promise you with everything that is in me, I am yours. Forever."

"I have another protégé," Irene said. "She's a sculptor from Santa Barbara. On this last trip I made her an offer and she accepted. She's moving to New York next week."

Henry threw the key at Irene's feet and left without another word.

"That's why we need a little more this month, Henry."

Henry was only half-listening to Mike and his excuses. He was more intent on finding something to drink. He filled a trashcan with the empty bottles of whiskey, beer, and wine on the counter and started rummaging through the pantry. There had to be something.

"How much?" Henry asked.

"A thousand."

Mike and his mother were off Basic Living and fully supported by Henry. He had bought them a modest home in Washington, D.C. and made monthly deposits to his mother's Index.

Henry found a bottle of amaretto. He gulped down half of what was left. "I'm not going to keep doing this, Mike. You have to figure out how to live on what I give you. It's more than enough."

"We were just having a little fun is all," Mike said. "Your mom needed a vacation. She hasn't been feeling so good, lately."

"Hasn't been feeling good how?" Henry finished the bottle of amaretto.

"Just aches and pains," Mike said. "The usual stuff."

"Take her to the doctor," Henry said. "She might need

medicine." Prolonged bliss usage had consequences. Henry had seen it in other people in the ward. People who were hollowed out, aged beyond their years. Henry's mom was no different.

"Yeah, I will," Mike promised. "About that thousand?"

"I'll send it today." Henry dropped the empty bottle in the trash.

"Thanks, Henry. You're a good son."

Henry called the liquor store down the street and asked for his usual order. Thirty minutes later, a young man showed up at his door with a brown cardboard box filled with a variety of alcoholic beverages.

"Thanks," Henry said, giving his thumbprint to the delivery boy.

"You're the artist, right?"

"That's me," he said.

"What are you working on now?"

"Top secret," Henry said. "I can't talk about it." He shut the door, putting the cardboard box on the dining room table. He selected an icy bottle of vodka and poured some into a glass. "Top secret," he said to himself, shaking his head. Henry drank enough to pass out. Enough to black out his memories of Irene. Enough to forget the blank canvases in his studio and the fact that he hadn't painted in months.

Irene had reached out to him multiple times after she ended their marriage, but Henry refused to answer the phone and avoided all social situations where he might run into her. He had come across Irene only once by accident. It had been through the window of a restaurant while he was eating lunch. Irene was walking by, arm in arm with a stunning girl with icy blonde hair. Henry knew it had to be her protégé. He had gone to the bathroom and vomited.

Henry hated that he couldn't paint anymore, but nothing came to him. His cynical side figured a scarcity of his work would just drive up prices, but the rest of him was terrified that the art world would simply move on. That he would squander what Irene had given him. Henry tried to fuck away his memory of Irene. It didn't work. He had no lack of willing bedmates, but as he drank more and more, he found that he was unable to meet his coital obligations. So Henry retreated to his lavish apartment and dedicated himself to the art of drinking.

"Wake up," the voice said.

Henry felt the light through his eyelids like stabbing knives. "Go away," he said.

"I ain't going anywhere," the voice said firmly. Henry recognized it.

"Mom?" Henry tried to sit up. He was still fairly drunk and his head was on fire. "What are you doing here?"

"You not answering your phone," she said, putting a glass of water in his hands. "Drink this."

"How much do you want this time?" Henry croaked.

"I ain't here for money," she said. "I'm here for you. I never thought you'd end up like this, Henry."

"End up like what? Achieving worldwide fame as the 'artist of his generation'?" This was according to a recent profile in TIME.

"You know what I mean."

"Say it."

"You've got a problem, Henry. You gonna kill yourself drinking like this. You gonna kill your art."

"You're the addict, Mom, not me."

"Takes one to know one."

"Just leave me alone." Henry stumbled to the kitchen sink and stuck his head under the faucet.

His mother followed. "You need to get help, Henry. I ain't leaving until you get it."

"You're so full of shit," Henry exploded. He dried his face off with a dish towel. "You're the one who needs help, not me. You're the one who used to whore yourself out for enough bliss to get through the day."

His mother slapped him across the face.

Henry took the blow, but didn't back down. "You can't come here, trying to tell me how to live my life. You've got no right. Not after what you've done."

"You weren't supposed to know," his mother said.

"I'm not stupid. I figured it out pretty fast. I only went to Keller to get you out of that life. You don't take care of me. I take care of you."

"You done got me out, Henry. You done more with your life than I ever coulda dreamed. Don't mess it up over some woman. She ain't worth it."

"I love her."

"You gotta harden that heart," his mother said. "You always felt stuff so strong. Like me, I guess. Don't make my mistakes, Henry. When your father left us, it seemed so dark all the time. Bliss helped make it better. I didn't want to stop. When it got to the bad times, I couldn't stop. You going to Keller was like things looking up for our family. You're not so far gone. You can get better."

"I don't want to get better."

"I don't believe you," she said. "I called Scott."

"What?"

"After I found you here. He's flying up from Atlanta. Gets in tonight. He got calls in to some of the best rehabs in

New York. You just gotta go with him."

"I don't need rehab, Mom."

"I said that too."

"I'll transfer ten grand to your Index right now if you tell Scott it was a mistake and leave."

"You can't buy me off."

"Then I'll cut you off." Henry said it coldly.

"I was on BL a long time," his mother replied. "I'll go back if it means you get the help you need."

"Mike won't stand for that."

"Mike ain't my blood."

Henry and his mother glared at each other, but he wilted under her stern resolve.

"I just want her back," Henry said, slumping down on the couch.

"You think she wants a pathetic drunk like you?" His mother's voice grew harsh. "You want her back then you get your fucking act together. You figure out why she left you and get her back."

"What if she turns me down?"

"Then you move on. You can't be with someone who don't want to be with you, Henry. Like trying to hold onto the wind."

Henry knew she wasn't talking about Irene anymore. When Scott arrived that night, Henry let him pour every bottle of liquor down the drain. In the morning, wanting nothing more than a drink, Henry went to rehab.

Henry had been sober for ninety-three days. He went to meetings twice a week. Scott called almost every day. So did his mother. He had turned to his work with a manic focus. One painting. Irene's portrait. It was part of their business agreement and the only thing he still owed her.

During the three years of their marriage, Henry had burned a dozen failed attempts to paint Irene. The setting was wrong. The pose was wrong. The medium was wrong. Now Henry painted like never before, mixing oil paint and strips of patterned cloth in a way that made his portrait come alive.

When Henry finished he felt whole. Somehow, in the creation of his final gift to Irene, he had healed. He knew that no matter what Irene decided, he would survive. It was in this frame of mind that he called her.

"Henry? It's so good to hear your voice." She sounded sincere. "How are you?"

"I'm doing well," he said. "I finished your portrait."

"That's great!" she said. "I can't wait to see it. When can you bring it by?"

"How about now?"

"Now would be fine," she said. "I'm free until two."

Henry carefully packaged the painting and took a cab to Irene's apartment. The doorman was new, and Henry had to give a thumbprint before the guy would let him up the elevator.

Irene answered the door on the first knock. She was wearing a tennis skirt and a tank top. "Come on in," she said.

Henry carried the painting into the room and leaned it against the wall. He started to undo the cardboard covering.

"Can I get you anything to drink?" Irene asked. "A beer?"

"No thanks," Henry said.

"I've missed you," she said. "I didn't think you would be so angry with me. I'm glad you reached out. I'm glad you're here." She watched him strip away some packing tape. "You look a little thin to me, you need to make sure you eat enough. You know how you get when you're working."

Henry removed the cardboard and began undoing the bubble wrap.

"Katrine is in Los Angeles for the week," Irene said. "That one has boundless energy."

Henry pulled off the last layer of plastic that protected the painting and oriented it the proper way. He stepped to the side, letting Irene come forward to see it.

She stared, speechless for several minutes.

"Do you like it?" Henry asked.

"Why did you do this?" Irene asked. "Why?"

"It's our future, Irene. If you want it."

"It's impossible," she whispered.

"It's not. Technology has come a long way in twenty years. I've done the research." Henry dropped to one knee, taking a ring out of his pocket. "I will never stop loving you. I want to build a life with you. I want to marry you. Permanently. No contract, no terms. You can even keep Katrine. A hundred Katrines. I don't care. Irene Morris, will you marry me?"

Irene looked at Henry. Then she looked at the painting. It was of Irene cradling a beautiful brown baby. She was in turn held by Henry.

"Yes," she said, with tears in her eyes. "Yes."

VERA AND BOB

There is only so much we can do to help them. At some point, they must help themselves.

Senator Ronald Harper, R Delaware, in opposition to the Basic Living Act, 12/3/34.

"How sold is the 8:30 showing of Tidings of Madness?" asked the young woman. She was in her early twenties, accompanied by a man about the same age. They were holding hands.

"About half full," Vera said. "We've got it playing at 9:45 and that's only ten percent full." She flipped the image around to show them.

"That's kind of late," the woman said.

"Agreed," said the guy. "How about that new romcom?"

"The reviews are terrible," the woman said. "If we're going to see Alana Baxter, I want to see her as Jenna Bond. What seats are available for 8:30?"

Vera pulled up the chart.

"That's not bad," the woman said. "How about those

two?"

"Looks good to me," the guy said.

Vera touched both seats and the guy pressed his thumb in the payment square. "You're in Theater 8," Vera said. "Enjoy the show!"

The couple got in line for concessions. Bob was working the popcorn machine. He always smelled a bit like popcorn these days. They had gotten part-time jobs quite easily through the Intergen program. They worked twenty hours a week, which was the most they were allowed under the stipend conditions.

It was enough to help out with food and household bills, with some left over for them to make their small garage space more homey. Bob cut and framed a few windows, finished drywalling and painted the walls a sunny shade of yellow. They borrowed Chris's truck on trash days for the wealthier parts of town and checked sidewalks for good discards. This netted them a table, chairs and a small couch that Vera reupholstered with fabric she found on clearance. She made curtains too and they bought a larger rug at a thrift store.

Vera helped Jolene with the daycare and Bob fixed things around the house and did some gardening. The landlady was really impressed with his work and started giving him odd jobs at her other properties. Jolene claimed it was because he was cheaper than the professionals, but Bob didn't care. He liked keeping busy and it was nice to have the extra cash.

Vera sold a group of teenagers tickets to an action movie with fast cars. Vera hadn't cared for that one. Call her old-fashioned, but she thought women should wear more clothes than that. She had really enjoyed the Alana Baxter romantic comedy that the young woman had spurned. It was about a married couple, both lawyers, who were on opposite sides of a hysterically nasty divorce case. She was pretty sure it was a remake. Vera and Bob got to watch as many movies as they wanted for free, and often came to work early to catch a matinee together. It was her favorite part of the job. After work, they caught the bus home, though there was one manager who insisted on giving them rides whenever they worked the same nights.

Even when they didn't get off until midnight, Vera and Bob woke up fairly early. They purchased a used refrigerator and kept it stocked with breakfast food so they wouldn't disturb Jolene's family. Of course, they had to come in whenever they needed the bathroom, but they tried to be as unobtrusive as possible.

In the evenings, Vera made dinner whenever she didn't have to work and always assisted with clean up. Afterward, she and Bob would give little Rosie kisses goodnight and go right back to their room. They figured they should give Jolene and Chris as much space as possible. Seven months into the new living situation, Jolene took Vera aside and told her it was going great. She and Chris really appreciated all of their help and were able to put every dime of the stipends into their down payment fund. Jolene expected them to be able to purchase their own place in a few years.

"We should do something to help Bob, Jr.," Vera said. She was feeling quite content with life. Jolene was expecting a second child, they were looking at houses with a realtor, and Bob, Jr. was due to be released from prison in a week. As part of his release, he would get to live in a halfway house rent-free for six months. The biggest problem would be finding work. Vera liked solving problems.

"There isn't much we can do," Bob said. They were on

the bus to the movie theater. The hard plastic seats made Vera's back ache, but at least it was clean. The city had passed a bunch of ordinances to encourage tourism. These included strict rules to preserve Nashville's new fleet of solar-painted buses. No eating, drinking, or gum. Offenders were suspended for a week or more. Vandals were banned for a year. For people who had no other way of getting around the city, this provided all the incentive needed to support the "Nashville's Neat!" campaign.

"What if we talk to Matthew?" she asked. Matthew was the nice manager who gave them rides home. "We could ask him to give Bob, Jr. a job when he gets out."

"It's all part-time work for elderly folk and pimply teens," Bob said. "There aren't any full-time jobs."

"He doesn't need one right away," Vera pointed out. "Part-time would be good enough, and if he works hard, then maybe Matthew could give him a recommendation or promote him if a full-time position opens up."

"That's an idea," Bob said, "if Matthew even gives him a chance. But what if Bob, Jr. slacks off or gets caught stealing? It could put our jobs in trouble."

"He wouldn't do anything like that. Not if he knew it could hurt us."

"You've got to be realistic, Vera. Bob, Jr. doesn't have a record of making good decisions."

"He's learned his lesson. This is the longest he's ever been in prison. He said he never wants to go back. He doesn't want to end up tractabilized."

"What's that?"

"It's what they do to those prisoners who refuse to work. Bob, Jr. got up the courage to ask one of the guards about it. It's some kind of implant. It makes you obey, so that's why the guys don't come back. They go to a different prison that's all tractiles. That's what he called them."

"Makes you obey how? And who?"

"I don't know," Vera said. "I think it just numbs that part of your brain that questions authority."

"So if I told a tractile to jump off a building, he would?"

"I don't know," Vera said.

"That doesn't sound right to me."

"They only do it to the worst guys, the ones who are in prison for life anyway. But I guess there are rumors about turning the whole prison population into tractiles."

"Are you sure that guard wasn't pulling Bob, Jr.'s leg?"

"I guess he could have been," Vera said. "But nothing sounds too crazy to me these days. The world's a different place than it once was."

"You can say that again," Bob said. "Let's talk to Bob, Jr. before we ask Matthew about the job. He may not even want to work at the movie theater."

"Alright," Vera said.

G.M. WHITLEY

MARI AND VICTOR

Why must they keep increasing taxes on the so-called rich? Darling Chester may have to go to a less expensive private school and I don't know how we'll still afford Lupe to care for little Tulle. I might have to resign from the board of The Ladies Who Lunch Wearing Pearls Charity and take care of her myself! Dear God what will people at the club think? It won't matter, because we won't even be members of the club anymore. Our delightfully large and well-appointed home is just so expensive to maintain and the mortgage is enormous. How can we keep paying for our gardener and housekeeper?

We don't live extravagantly by any means. Many Americans have gardeners, housekeepers, and nannies and struggle to get by, just like us. It isn't fair. This law is going to put good people out of work. People like Lupe the Nanny, Hector the Gardener, and — what is our housekeeper's name again? I forget. She's a new one, the last one never got the baseboards clean. Anyway, why should I have to give up any of my husband's hard-earned money to pay for the government's decision to provide handouts to the unwashed masses? What is the world coming to?

Excerpt from The Rich Woman's Lament, Op-Ed, New York Times, 7/15/35.

After the implantation, Mari was put on forty-eight hours of bed rest in the labor and delivery wing of the farm. After Alyssa and the doctor left, Mari cried herself raw, screaming into her pillow to muffle the sound. When she heard a nurse come in to check on her, Mari held her breath and pretended to be asleep until the woman left. She mourned the loss of her baby all over again, reliving the night of blood and fear. She raged at what Cassie had done to her, pummeling her fists on the bed like a child throwing a tantrum. She cried from guilt and shame, wondering if she had subconsciously known what Cassie was doing. Had she noticed the lemonade was a little bitter? A little gritty? Was there a part of her that was glad that Cassie had taken the action she could not bring herself to take? Mari couldn't allow herself to think like that and instead focused on her anger. When Brandy knocked on her door with two trays of food a few hours later, Mari's eyes were red but dry.

"This is the boring part," Brandy said, setting a tray on Mari's nightstand and sitting in the chair next to the bed. "Then again how often do you get to stay in bed all day and watch TV?" Brandy noticed that Mari had been crying. "Are you OK? You shouldn't be hormonal yet."

"Did you know?" Mari asked, keeping her voice calm and controlled.

"Did I know what?"

"What Cassie did to me."

"What are you talking about?" Brandy looked genuinely bewildered.

"There is no way an embryo transfer would have worked," Mari hissed. "Alyssa and I talked about it at lunch. It takes six weeks to recover and leaves a scar. Cassie was bullshitting me. Buying time. Keeping me quiet. She drugged me, Brandy. She killed my baby."

"You're talking crazy," Brandy said.

"Did you know?"

"How can you ask me something like that?" Brandy started to get up.

Mari leaned forward and pushed her back with both hands. "You knew."

"Watch yourself, Mari," Brandy warned, standing up. "This crazy is between you and Cassie. Freak out on her and leave me out of it."

"You had to know."

"What do you want from me?"

"The truth!"

"The truth is I didn't know about embryo transfer anymore than you did. Nobody I knew ever did one. I looked it up after you miscarried. It was too much of a coincidence."

"Why didn't you tell me?"

"What good would that have done? It was too late. Besides, you can't prove anything, Mari. Maybe Cassie didn't know about embryo transfer anymore than we did. It was like a false hope for her too. Then the miscarriage happened and it didn't matter anymore."

"I have to know."

"Then ask her when you get out of here."

"Oh I will."

"You know what, Mari? In the end, whatever Cassie did or didn't do, your life was ruined and now it isn't. And you didn't do anything wrong to get there."

"You're pregnant!" The doctor smiled at her. "Congratulations, Mari."

"Thanks," she said. Mari was very glad the implantation

had taken the first time. She felt safe now. With a baby in her, she was at her most valuable to the farm.

"You'll be coming in every week for check-ups," the doctor said. "You might start feeling nauseated in a few weeks. If you can't keep anything down, we'll hook you up to an IV with fluids and nutrients. We've got some girls in every day for that. You aren't approved for any drugs, so you'll just have to deal with morning sickness. Do you have any questions?"

"No," Mari said. "Can I go now?"

"Of course," the doctor said.

Mari went straight to Cassie's room and knocked on the door. There was no answer. She knocked again and again, until another chaperone came out of the room next door. "What are you doing?" she asked.

"Where's Cassie?" Mari asked, as casually as she could. "I haven't seen her around."

"She retired," the woman said. "Moved out yesterday."

"Where?" Mari asked.

"I think she went to live with her son in Victorville."

"Why?"

"I don't know. She put in her notice almost a month ago. We've got someone new moving in next week after they get her place cleaned and repainted."

Mari went back to her room and Indexed Cassie. Her phone number was not public, but she had an email address. Mari sent her a short message. "I know what you did."

She never got a response.

"There it is again!" Alyssa gave a delighted laugh. Her hands were pressed to Mari's bare belly. "Maybe she'll be a soccer player!"

Mari smiled. It was best to let Alyssa do most of the

talking. She had come in for each monthly sonogram, alone. Mari stopped asking about her husband and Alyssa stopped volunteering excuses. Instead, she talked about all the preparations she was making for the baby. All the books she was reading on childrearing.

"I had the room painted," Alyssa said. "I hired an artist to do a mural. It's a jungle theme. I wanted to keep it gender neutral since I think we'll have a boy next time." Alyssa showed Mari a few pictures on her phone. "My mother sent us a crib and my mother-in-law could not be outdone so she sent us the dresser and a changing table. Drake made that rocking chair with the cushions, remember him? He's hosting the baby shower next month. We're doing a champagne brunch!"

"Sounds wonderful," Mari said.

"How are you doing? How is school?" This was the question Alyssa always asked.

"Great," Mari said. "It's still going really well." Mari had been accepted to Cal State Los Angeles to study elementary education. She was taking an intensive course online, spending half the day listening to lectures and the other half studying. As soon as she passed the final exam, she could move on to the next one. Mari wasn't a natural student, and it was a struggle at times to stay focused. But every time she felt like delaying a lecture or skipping her reading, Mari looked at Cassie's Index. The woman was content in retirement, playing with grandchildren and planting vegetables in her son's yard according to the photos. It was infuriating. Mari channeled her anger into her studies. She was determined to be successful. Her baby's death wouldn't be for nothing. With no distractions and the regimented schedule of the farm, Mari was already four classes in and on target to finish her degree in three years. "I've gotten all A's so far," Mari added.

"That's fantastic," Alyssa said. "School should be your top priority. Other than taking care of this little one, of course."

"Of course," Mari echoed. She felt a particularly strong kick.

"Definitely soccer," Alyssa said, taking her hands off Mari's stomach.

The doctor walked in holding Mari's chart. "Ready for the sonogram, ladies?"

"Can't wait," Alyssa said.

"I'm so ready for this baby to be out," Mari said. "I wonder if Alyssa's husband is going to make it. I'm starting to think she made him up. Either that or he's a total asshole."

Brandy shrugged. "The guys are never as involved," she said. "They give the sperm and their job is done. Guys don't like to feel unnecessary. Fatherhood isn't really their thing until the kid is old enough to catch a ball. That's how my dad was, anyway. Birth is the big photo-op though, so I'm guessing he'll be there." Brandy peeled a banana and took a bite. "Being pregnant makes me so hungry."

"I can't believe you never get morning sickness," Mari said. "Can you lie to me and tell me you hurled at least once in three pregnancies?"

"Not once," Brandy said, finishing the banana. "I'm good breeding stock."

"Bitch." Mari had suffered for six weeks, nauseated but never able to throw up.

"You love me. Gotta run. Prenatal massage time." Brandy winked. She was dating the cute masseuse. Mari tried not to think about what happened during those massage sessions. It made her think of her nights with Victor. It made her want him back.

Mari was hungry too, but couldn't eat until after the operation. She waddled down the hall toward the medical wing.

"Mari!" Alyssa called. She was standing with a man wearing horn-rimmed glasses. With Alyssa in low heels, they were about the same height. The man's stomach hung slightly over his pants and his cropped hair could not hide a growing baldness." This is my husband, Ben."

Mari hid her surprise. This was not how she had imagined him. She had thought he would look more like Drake, a tall and handsome match to Alyssa's carefully preserved beauty.

"Nice to finally meet you, Mari," he said, extending a hand. He spoke with a thick British accent. His handshake was firm and confident.

"Nice to meet you too," she said.

"I hear you are doing very well in school," he said.

"Yes," Mari said. Brandy said that all the parents were obsessed with their surrogates' education. It supposedly made them feel less guilty about exploiting poor girls barely out of high school and fresh off BL.

"Well, when it comes time for you to find a job, you let us know. I play poker with the Superintendent of Schools for Los Angeles County. I'm sure we could get your resume to the top of the stack." Ben smiled at her, his blue eyes twinkling behind his glasses.

"Thank you," Mari said, deciding that Ben was more attractive than he first appeared.

"I don't think Alyssa's had a chance to talk with you about this, but we plan to reserve you," Ben said. "For our next one. We'd also like you to provide breast milk for this one, if you can. It's supposed to be better fresh instead of processed through a milk bank. It should let you put a little away after you've paid tuition. What do you think?"

"Sounds great," Mari said. It would be steady income, both from the milk and from forgoing other opportunities to surrogate.

"We already talked with your liaison about it," Alyssa said. "We'll tell the nurse to put a pump in your recovery room. You'll need to start pumping right away even if you only get a few drops. The colostrum is really important."

"OK," Mari said.

"Well then, let's get our baby out of you, why don't we?" Ben said, leading them to the nurse's station.

Mari was awake for the whole procedure. She felt no pain, but did experience a tugging sensation as the doctor pulled the baby from her womb. She heard a cry and caught a brief glimpse of the child as she was toweled off and taken to an incubator. Alyssa and her husband trailed after the nurse.

Mari felt more tugging as the doctor closed the incision. She watched a wrapped bundle being placed in Alyssa's arms. Alyssa was crying and her husband had his arms around her. Mari thought she could see tears in his eyes too and it made her happy for them. Then she thought of her lost baby, of her and Victor holding an infant girl in their arms. She began crying, the tears falling silently from her eyes.

"Does it hurt, Mari?" the doctor asked with concern. "You're looking great. We've got a clean closure that should hardly leave a scar."

"I'm fine. Just happy," Mari lied.

The doctor accepted the lie and turned away to talk to the nurse.

"Look!" Alyssa brought the bundle over and showed it to Mari.

Mari wiped her tears away and saw a scrunched red face with dark eyes under a pink knit cap. The baby had stopped crying.

"She's beautiful," Mari said.

"Are you up for visitors?" the nurse asked.

"Yes!" Mari said. "I'm almost done pumping. Five minutes?"

"I'll let them know," the nurse said.

Mari's mother had called to let her know she was going to take the train with Marcus right after she finished work. Mari was excited to see them. It felt strange to have the baby gone. Lonely, somehow. Mari turned the pump off. There was a tiny bit of liquid in the bottom of each bottle.

The nurse came back. "How did you do?" she asked, squinting at the bottles. "That's great!" she exclaimed, taking a feeding syringe out of her pocket. She sucked the colostrum up. "You got six milliliters! I'll take this to the baby right away." The nurse bustled out of the room. Mari pulled her shirt down and put the dirty bottles and flanges in the sink. She was rinsing them out when she heard her mother's voice.

"We're here!" she said brightly.

Mari turned around, leaning against the sink. Marcus was standing next to their mother. Behind her, his face obscured by the large vase of flowers, was Victor. Mari's hand slipped from the counter and she stumbled back.

"Oh, sweetheart," her mother said, "you shouldn't be up. Let a nurse wash those bottles." Mari was bustled back into bed.

"Where's the baby?" Marcus asked.

"With her mommy and daddy."

"Can I see where the doctor cut you?"

"No. It's all bandaged up right now." Marcus continued to pepper her with questions. Mari answered them all, keeping an eye on Victor. He set the vase on the counter. Then he moved it to the table at the foot of her bed. After a minute, he picked it up again and set it on the windowsill.

"You can just leave it there," Mari said loudly, interrupting Marcus's next question, which was whether or not the baby was his sister.

"Sorry," Victor mumbled, shoving his hands into the pockets of his jacket. "I'll just go."

"No, don't," Mari said. "I mean, thank you for the flowers. They are beautiful."

Marcus tried to ask his question again.

"Hey Marcus!" Mari's mother said, "Let's see what they got at the vending machines. Uncle Victor gave me a few dollars." She held up three golden coins.

"Yippee!" Marcus said, running out of the room.

Mari's mother went after him. "You two work this out, OK?" she called over her shoulder.

"So," Victor said. "I'm sorry."

"You've said that before."

"I shouldn't have lied to you."

"You've said that before, too."

"I miss you, Mari. I love you. I'm ready to wait for you."

As he spoke, Mari realized she was no longer angry with him. Victor was Victor and she loved him in spite of it all. He was dedicated to her. "Cassie's gone," she said. "Retired. You can't be with me that way. Can you handle that?"

"It's better than not being with you at all," he said. "Please, Mari. Please?" Victor took her hand and kissed her knuckles.

Mari sighed, her whole body tingling.

Victor gave a triumphant growl and kissed her, careful not to press against her stitches. Mari returned his kiss with enthusiasm. It went on for some time, growing more heated, until a young voice came from the doorway.

"Gross!" Marcus exclaimed, a half-eaten candy bar in one hand.

Victor hastily pulled back and Mari laughed her first real laugh in months.

JEREMY AND RACHEL

Candace is 35 and a single waitress/actress/model/singer/personal trainer. She longs to meet "the one" and raise fat babies.

Lesley is 37 and a married stay at home mother with advanced degrees and three children under the age of 5. She is tired of wrangling kids all day.

Enter Life Swap.

Paul is 20 and a undecided sophomore at Florida State University. He has never worked a day in his life, parties seven nights a week and is flunking out of school. His parents are about to cut him off.

Ian is 19 and on Basic Living. He spends half the week cleaning algae bioreactors and the other half training to be a mechanic. His work ethic has earned him a corporate sponsor.

Enter Life Swap.

Is the grass always greener? Tune in and find out!

Harvey Samuels Broadcasting Network Teaser for Life Swap, Series Premiere, 9/4/2074.

Jeremy couldn't sleep. He compulsively checked his emails to see if any of the lawyers had responded. Three hours into the flight to Atlanta, he heard from two in quick succession. One asked for a twenty thousand dollar retainer and promised to get started first thing Monday morning. The other wanted more details about his sister's condition and would only take the case if her prognosis was better than fifty percent. Jeremy decided to wait for one of the others to respond and instead contacted all the clinical trials that might take Rachel.

He read every case he could find on guardianship and Basic Living. The closest one was a child who had also been denied treatment on BL and an older sister tried to obtain guardianship. The sister's insurance company tried to stop it, claiming that the guardianship was in name only, so that the child would receive coverage. The court allowed the guardianship to transfer after the sister showed the provisions she had made for the child to live in her home and the enrollment forms she had filed with the local elementary school. Jeremy started looking at apartments near the Marietta Enclave. Grier surely wouldn't let Rachel live in the assistant suite.

When he had done all that he could, Jeremy's thoughts turned to Grier's wife. That poor woman, forced to wait until her husband and caregivers were away long enough for her to try to kill herself. It went against everything Jeremy had learned in Peace Out Education. He marveled at the cruelty of denying a grown woman the right to end her life gracefully.

Rachel was an entirely different situation, Jeremy thought. Someone so young should never give up, should never stop fighting. Jeremy wanted to see her graduate from high school. He wanted to help her go to college and maybe someday walk her down the aisle. Rachel deserved life.

As soon as the plane stopped at the gate, Jeremy rushed to the taxi stand. He had just enough time to get to the hospital and stop the transfer to Peace Out. "Atlanta Children's, please," he said, hopping into the next available cab.

"You got it." The driver went back to talking on his phone and pulled into traffic.

"Please hurry."

"Always do," the man drawled.

Jeremy checked his messages again. Three more attorneys had responded. Two wanted large retainers. The last had reviewed Rachel's Gift of Life page and declined to represent him. Jeremy started researching self-representation. When he arrived at the hospital, he went straight to Rachel's room, a copy of the temporary restraining order form in hand.

"Jeremy!" his mother said, clinging to him. Jeremy pressed her to his chest, his chin resting on the top of her head, feeling her tears dampen his shirt. He looked past her to the small figure in the bed, dotted with electrodes and hooked up to several machines. Jeremy let go of his mother and went to his sister.

"Rachel?" he asked.

She opened her eyes and gave him a faint smile. She was skeletal, her eyes sunken and her skin grey. Her legs were in casts up to her hips.

"What happened?" he whispered.

"She had a seizure in the night," his mother answered. "Both femurs snapped. Her bones are just," his mother's voice caught and she cleared her throat, "they're disintegrating."

Jeremy reached out to caress Rachel's cheek. Her eyes widened.

"Stop!" His mother cried.

Jeremy's hand froze, inches away.

"Don't touch her. It hurts too much, even with bliss."

Jeremy slowly folded up the paper in his hands and put it in his pocket. He squared his shoulders. "When is she transferring to Peace Out?"

"She's not," his mother sighed. "They said moving her would kill her."

"OK." Jeremy planted himself in the chair next to Rachel's bed. "Hey kiddo, I was just in San Francisco. Want to hear about it?"

Rachel's lips turned up slightly.

Jeremy started talking, showing her pictures of the Golden Gate Bridge, the hilly streets, and quaint houses. His mother pulled up a chair next to him. He talked about the ride on the private jet. He talked about the Easter baskets that he had made for Grier's grandchildren, packed with robotic animal companions, egg-shaped chalk from Paris, and first editions of rare children's books for the younger ones. The older ones got designer sunglasses. Each girl received a platinum necklace with a yellow diamond encrusted pendant from Harry Winston and the boys all received old-fashioned pocket watches with lots of gears, handmade by an artisan in London.

"But I saved the best for you," Jeremy continued. He reached into his bag and took out a brown and white stuffed bunny and a beautifully illustrated copy of The Velveteen Rabbit. "I'll just put him right here," he said, setting the bunny on the bedside table. "Do you want me to read the story?"

Rachel gave the tiniest nod. A nurse came in while he was reading and replaced the various bags of liquid hooked to Rachel. Jeremy kept talking, telling Rachel all about Paige and how she saved the day with the Easter baskets. Rachel liked hearing about silly Mr. Grier, which was how Jeremy always couched his stories about Grier's sometimes ludicrous demands. He told her he had promised Paige that they would take her to barbeque the next time she was in Atlanta. He told Rachel how much he loved her. He talked until his voice was hoarse.

While Jeremy was telling Rachel about room service, where someone would bring whatever you ordered right to you, even an ice cream sundae, Rachel closed her eyes and died. His mother threw herself on the body, sobbing, while Jeremy watched, dry-eyed. He held his mother while the doctor called the time of death. He spoke to the local mortuary and contacted a deacon about funeral arrangements for the next weekend. One of the deacon's wives came to the hospital and offered his mother a room in their home for a few nights so she wouldn't be alone.

Leaving his mother in the hands of the kindly woman with a promise to come over for dinner, Jeremy went back to the Marietta Enclave. He worked his way through a backlog of emails for Grier, then contacted all the attorneys and clinical trials, informing them that his sister had passed. He updated Rachel's Gift of Life page, thanking all the donors for their support. Then he called Paige.

"I'm so sorry," she said. "How is your mother?"

"Devastated," he said. "Heartbroken."

"How are you?"

"I'm fine," Jeremy said.

"Are you sure?" she asked.

"I really am. It's almost a relief, you know," he said. "She was so sick. She's in a better place."

"It's OK to grieve," Paige said. "It's OK to be angry and upset."

"I don't feel that way at all, though," Jeremy said. "Trust me, I've already tried to figure out why. Maybe I'm in shock and I'll fall apart any minute. But I really think it is because I did my grieving a long time ago. In a way, I'm grateful to feel nothing right now. It means I can handle things for my mother and stay on top of my job."

"Well, I've got things under control here," Paige said. "I dropped Grier off at his brownstone late last night. His house manager helped me get him to bed without waking his daughter and grandkids. He's still sleeping it off. I pushed all his calls and meetings to Monday. Nothing was urgent."

"Thank you, Paige," Jeremy said. "Did he throw up?"

"On a patch of grass in front of his house. When I stopped by this morning to check on him, it was already starting to turn brown." Paige laughed. "It must be quite a unique experience, working for him."

"He's got his flaws, but Mr. Grier is a good man," Jeremy said. "He paid for most of Rachel's chemotherapy."

"I'm sorry," Paige said hastily. "I hope I didn't offend. I think it's really amazing that Mr. Grier did that for you. You guys must have a very close relationship."

"I'm sorry, too," Jeremy said. "I shouldn't have jumped down your throat. I guess I must be more on edge than I realized. I really appreciate everything you've done for me. Hopefully I can take you out on a real date after I fly back tomorrow."

"I would like that," Paige said. "See you soon."

This time, Jeremy fell asleep after take-off and woke to the sound of a flight attendant's cheerful yet insistent voice. When he opened his eyes, the woman flashed a pure white set of veneers and told him they had arrived in San Francisco and would he please deplane so they could prep the aircraft for their next departure. Jeremy apologized and took a cab to the hotel. He sent Grier a message letting him know he was back. Grier called less then a minute later.

Jeremy heard the happy shrieks of children in the background. Grier offered a perfunctory statement about his heart going out to Jeremy and his mother in this difficult time, and asked Jeremy to send a large bouquet of flowers to the service on his behalf. He thanked Jeremy for the Easter baskets. The children, big and small, had simply adored them. He also told Jeremy to do no work for the rest of the day, so Jeremy called Paige.

They went to an Italian restaurant and shared a bottle of wine. Then they went back to Jeremy's hotel room and watched a movie. Jeremy asked Paige to stay the night and she did. They fell asleep fully clothed, holding hands.

In the morning, Jeremy and Paige awoke to the ringing of their phones. She practically ran back to her hotel room to get ready and Jeremy took phone calls and answered emails while using the bathroom, shaving, and brushing his teeth. At the office, they barely had a chance to say hello before they were pinged with more requests. Jeremy saw Paige wolfing down an AlgiProtein bar in the lobby around noon, but was too busy to join her. She waved at him while he inhaled a stale sandwich from a vending machine a few hours later and then disappeared into a conference room.

Toward the end of the day, when Jeremy was finishing up in the restroom, washing his hands, Grier's son came in. "It's Jeremy, right?" he asked.

"Yes, Mr. Grier," Jeremy said.

"Call me David," he said. David's dark brown hair had a sprinkle of silver at the temples. He wore a tailored grey suit that definitely didn't come off a rack and his brown leather wingtips were spotless.

"Sure," Jeremy said.

"I'm so sorry for your loss," he said. "It must be so hard, having to work today."

"It keeps me occupied," Jeremy said.

"You've worked with my father for some time now," David said. "He trusts you. I can see that." David paused. "We were never close, my father and I. He was always working, and when he was there he seemed to care most about my grades and beating me on the tennis court. Dad raised me to take over the family business someday, but now that the day is coming closer, he won't let go. He really hasn't been the same since my mother died." David waited for Jeremy to say something. Jeremy just dried his hands and tossed the used paper towel in the trash.

"I'm concerned about his health," David continued, "the stress of this job. I know all about his drinking. He's not a young guy anymore. His body can't take this behavior."

"Have you tried talking with him about it?" Jeremy finally asked.

"You rescheduled our call five times in the past month," David retorted. "I've tried."

"He's here now. You're here now."

"He won't give me a minute alone with him."

"What do you want from me?"

"Could you keep an eye on him? Just let me know how he is doing every week or so? I can pay you for your time."

"Are you truly concerned for your father's well-being or are you looking for an excuse to remove him from his position?"

"What?"

Jeremy repeated his question.

"Is that what he thinks I'm trying to do?" David asked incredulously. "Good God, can't a son show concern for his father?"

"Not with a multi-billion dollar company at stake, apparently. You were the one just talking about his inability to let go." Jeremy felt strange but good, speaking with such confident insolence to such an important man.

If David was offended, he didn't show it. "Dad's going to be President and CEO as long as he wants the job. No one is questioning that. But there is no reason for him to work so hard when he has people underneath him to lighten the load. He's starting to micromanage. It's no way to run a company."

"It's his company," Jeremy said.

"I appreciate your loyalty," David said. "But this is really about what's best for my father and his legacy."

"I won't accept your money," Jeremy said. "It wouldn't be right."

"I understand," David said. He turned to leave.

"Wait," Jeremy said. "I never had the chance to be close to my father. He died when I was little. If your concern is genuine, then I will tell you where he is having breakfast tomorrow morning."

"Thank you," David said, turning back to shake Jeremy's hand.

Jeremy completed his executive assistant certificate in a year, making himself indispensable to Grier along the way. He was rewarded with an unexpectedly large bonus. Jeremy used most of it to pay off Rachel's outstanding medical bills and spent the rest on a weekend-long Atlantic City bachelor party for Tyler. He served as best man at Tyler and Shana's wedding,

Paige flying in from San Francisco to join him. They stayed in touch after that, but tacitly agreed that dating long-distance would not work.

When Jeremy let Grier know that his mother completed her secretarial coursework, he hired her to replace his retiring household manager in San Francisco. His mother was looking forward to the change in scenery. Jeremy was looking forward to an excuse to fly to San Francisco on a regular basis. A week before the move, Jeremy took the bus to the ward to help his mother pack.

"Would you help me go through Rachel's things?" she asked. "I can't do it alone."

"Sure, Mom," he said. Jeremy was proud of how he had coped with Rachel's death over the past year. He had given the eulogy at her funeral without shedding a tear. He had been strong for his mother. He had excelled at his job. He had accepted that she was gone.

The sight of her side of the small studio, untouched, left him unmoved. Everything Rachel owned was in a few boxes under her bed. Jeremy started setting things out while his mother divided them into piles for trash, donations, and keepsakes. He put all her clothes in one pile, the shabby hand-me-downs and the BL greys. The fancy dress he had bought had been cremated with her. He found a stack of schoolwork and put it in the trash pile. His mother noticed and started to flip through the papers. "She was a good student."

"I think she would have gotten sponsored," Jeremy said.

"I think so too," his mother agreed. She ruffled through the stack and stopped on a piece of pale blue construction paper. "I forgot about this," she said. "Rachel did it for school after she finished chemo. I think it would be nice for you to keep it." His mother handed him the paper.

It was a cartoonish drawing of Jeremy, wearing a superhero costume, complete with cape. He was holding hands with a beaming Rachel. She had attempted to draw the fancy dress and had given herself long brown hair, curling at her waist.

Jeremy wept.

EPILOGUE

Irene and Henry married on a secluded beach in Hawaii with only the minister and a photographer in attendance. Using the latest splicing technology, donor eggs, and a surrogate, Irene and Henry had two children, a girl and a boy. Henry paints a family portrait every year.

Henry supported his mother and Mike until his mother's death from multiple organ failure, a complication of long-term bliss usage. His mother lived long enough to meet her second grandchild and for her first grandchild to occasionally ask why Grandma died. Henry's attorney sent Mike a strongly worded letter and a final, significant check. Henry never heard from Mike again.

Henry served as best man in Scott's wedding, gifting him a painting of a busy New York street, packed with cars, people, buildings, and almost no sky. In stark contrast to the frenetic energy of the rest of the painting, the lower left-hand section featured two young men, one black, one white, sitting at an outdoor cafe table watching the world go by.

Vera and Bob convinced their manager to give Bob, Jr. a job after he got out of prison. The manager offered him a part-time position as a janitor and Bob, Jr. worked diligently. After his time in the halfway house was up, however, Bob, Jr. was unable to find full-time employment.

With Vera and Bob living in their garage and a second child on the way, Jolene and Chris could not let Bob, Jr. stay with them. So Bob, Jr. went on Basic Living, where he fulfills his work requirements as a custodian at the local junior high.

Vera and Bob continued to work at the movie theater and help Jolene with the daycare, their grandchildren, and the house. They did their best to be inconspicuous when they weren't needed. Chris and Jolene were able to purchase a small three-bedroom home with a large backyard in a decent school district by the time little Rosie was in second grade.

Bob died of a heart attack at 80. Vera died in her sleep six months later, on what would have been their fiftieth wedding anniversary.

Mari bore two more children for Alyssa and Ben. During that time she earned her BA and MA in Elementary Education. On Ben's recommendation, Mari got a job teaching sixth grade at the BL ward in Los Angeles. Mari went on Gel before leaving the farm and married Victor a month later.

Victor became frustrated that Mari earned more money than he did and had opinions on how they should be saving and spending. He began supplementing his income with illicit activities. Mari was unaware of this and went off Gel on their second wedding anniversary.

When their daughter was a year old, Victor was arrested and sentenced to five years in prison. Mari's mother and little brother moved in. Mari's mother took care of the baby while Mari supported all four of them. Mari divorced Victor while he was still in prison and gained full custody. She put their daughter on Gel when she turned fourteen.

Mari never remarried. Victor went back and forth between BL and jail for the rest of his life. She never told him about Cassie and the miscarriage. Their daughter earned a degree in environmental engineering and works for a consulting company.

Jeremy continued to work as Mr. Grier's personal assistant. He and Paige finally started dating long-distance, but neither would give up their job for the other. The breakup was amicable. Jeremy dated regularly after that, but his work schedule was too intense and unpredictable for a lasting relationship to develop.

Grier eventually reconciled with his son, though he refused to change anything about the way he ran AlgiPro. He also instituted a ten-year plan to transfer leadership of the company. Six years into the plan, Grier died on the operating table, just after receiving an outrageously expensive, specially cultivated liver to replace his damaged one.

David Grier offered Jeremy a job in San Francisco as executive assistant to the Chief Operating Officer of AlgiPro. Jeremy accepted and immediately contacted Paige. She was still single. They married in less than a year. Their second child was a daughter. They named her Rachel.

There will always be the poor. The question is what to do with them.

Senator Miriam Baxter, R Arizona, architect of the Basic Living Act, 5/14/28.

Questions and Topics for Discussion

1. Which storyline did you enjoy the most? The least? Why?
2. Do you think requiring reversible sterilization of BL recipients is right or wrong?
3. Is it right to impose work requirements on BL recipients?
4. What is your opinion of BL's voucher and points system?
5. Why do you think Mari stays with Victor?
6. Did Jeremy have a moral obligation to pay for his sister's cancer treatment?
7. Did Jolene have a moral obligation to care for Vera and Bob?
8. Was Henry's decision to accept Irene's offer the right one?
9. Would you be in favor or against a National Index?
10. Do you think a marriage system with term options is good or bad?
11. What is your opinion of Waverly Funding Services and using indentured servitude as collateral?
12. What is your view of surrogate farms as an alternative to traditional pregnancy?
13. Should Mari have voluntarily gotten an abortion?

ABOUT THE AUTHOR

G.M. Whitley is the Chief Operating Officer of the Whitley household, where she manages the lives of her husband and four young children. She taught at the University of Chicago and practiced intellectual property law in Los Angeles before accepting the amazing offer from her husband to serve as COO. She currently makes her home in Anchorage, Alaska.

Made in the USA
Charleston, SC
14 September 2013